Urban Tales

Charles Harvey

Published by Wes Writers and Publishers, 2024.

Urban Tales

by
Charles W. Harvey
PUBLISHED BY:
Wes Writers and Publishers
UrbanTales
Copyright © 2013 by Charles W. Harvey
Rev 2024 Two Poems Added

This is a work of fiction. Similarities to real people, places, or events are entirely coincidental.

URBAN TALES

First edition. February 24, 2024.

Copyright © 2024 Charles Harvey.

ISBN: 979-8224768561

Written by Charles Harvey.

Table of Contents

Urban Tales

Acknowledgements

All thanks to friends, and fans. I thank you for your praises and support.

Other Books[1]

---

1. https://charlesharveyauthor.wordpress.com/books/

The Stained Glass House

On his way home one morning from spending the night with one of the neighboring women, Easy passed an abandoned Church someone had vandalized. A board had been pried from the window, and half of the stained glass lay shattered on the ground. Intact was a white dove carrying an olive branch sitting atop a blue cross. Underneath the dove, a pair of outstretched hands reached toward its talons. Easy picked up shards of stained glass. Pieces of heads and arms appeared to be looking or reaching towards the sky. He thought of the shed in Aunt Trulla's yard.

That evening, he stood in the middle of the shed looking at an old bumper from a sixty-eight Impala, a push lawn mower missing a wheel, old suitcases, piles of magazines and an assortment of metal. He measured the room and imagined how a bed, nightstand, and chair might fit. He would have to run electricity to power a lamp, heater, and perhaps a microwave. Easy pounded the double wooden walls made from oak and reinforced with brick mortar. He found a hollow spot and took a sledgehammer to the wall until he had created a three-foot by a three-foot opening.

Late that night Easy slipped back to the church armed with a crowbar and a laundry sack. He pried the remaining piece of the window from the church and put it in the cotton bag along with the big pieces of stained glass he picked up from the ground. He hid the window under Aunt Trulla's porch and gave her the sack of broken glass. While Aunt Trulla spent hours trying to make sense of the hands clasped in prayer, pieces of faces—an eye, a nose, lips, and angel wings—Easy worked in the old shed. He cleaned, swept, and replaced rotted floorboards. He was grateful for the carpentry skills he picked up in the penitentiary the second time around.

Easy sat exhausted one evening after a long day of work in the shed. Cutting the hole for the skylight had worn him out. Sidney had been little help since he was half drunk and spent most of the time trying to have sex. Easy looked around for something to prop his feet on and noticed the big red suitcase in the corner of the shed. He had neglected to toss it out with the other trash when he cleaned out the shed. Curious, he decided to open it. He rifled through the old clothes and bills from stores he had never heard of. He went through the purses and collected seventy-eight cents in old coins from the sixties and seventies. The floor was littered with old bus transfers, business cards and funeral programs. One of the obituaries caught his eye. On the front was a young woman who favored Maura.

Stella Jackson
Sunrise November 2 1966 Sunset June 1999
Survived by Mother: Mamie, Mamie Jackson
Daughters: Myesha Jackson and Maura Jackson

He read a few more lines of the obituary before stuffing it back in the purse. He opened the black bag and ran his hand along the satin lining. He suddenly jerked his finger and noticed a thin red line across the fingertip where a piece of paper had sliced. Easy carefully unfolded the paper.

Missing Black Teen Girl 17
Myesha Jackson last seen at Vanguard High School
5'7" 110 lbs. Black Hair ... High Cheekbones

He looked at the photo of a smiling dark skin girl in a white dress trimmed in lace. Myesha appeared older than her thirteen years in the long below the knee dress. Her smile seemed far away as if she was looking across a large body of water. Easy folded the paper and put it in his pocket. He tossed all of the loose papers back into the suitcase and pushed it aside when he noticed a photograph on the floor. Easy looked at Marie and Helene and felt a sense of déjà vu. He tried to remember where he had seen the baby boy with the broad nose and tiny curled fist.

"Somewhere, somewhere," Easy said to himself as he thought. He sighed, turned, and caught his reflection in a piece of aluminum framing for the skylight. He suddenly stood straight up from the chair.

"*Look what your old no-good daddy left behind,*" Easy remembered his grandmother saying to him when he was a child. She was looking at the baby pictures of him and his siblings. The baby boy with broad nose slept with his finger wrapped tight around a grinning man's lit cigar. "I think he wanted to burn you up," His grandmother laughed.

At first, Maura denied knowing anything about the child. "Probably some bastard those two lesbians adopted."

"Why would they send a picture to you. I know goddamn well that's my kid. He look just like I did when I was a baby. I ought to beat your damn ass!" He drew his fist back to hit Maura.

Sidney cowered drunk in a corner. Aunt Trulla sprayed him in the face with a can of lilac-scented Peace Be Still deodorizer and peace-making spray. Easy coughed and rubbed his eyes. She took the photo from his hand and looked at it.

"His spirit is happy now. You won't feel no more darkness by your side," Aunt Trulla said to Maura "They done found each other." She nodded at Easy. "Father and son done found each other."

"I'm going to get my boy," Easy said slamming the screen door. "I'm going to get my boy and bring him to America. Ain't no lesbians going to raise my boy."

Easy grabbed a beer from the ice chest in the shed and sat on the porch drinking. He ran his finger over the baby's broad nose and touched his own. Easy looked like his daddy, and his child carried those genes. And his child's child would populate the earth with broad nose men. He knew he loved his daughter, but he also had a son. He would get his boy. He sprinted out to the shed and tore through the suitcase and purses looking for an envelope in which the picture might have arrived. He found nothing and sat in the middle of clothes and papers crying. He had no money, but if he had to Easy vowed, he would walk across the water and get his son. He drank and listened to music until the sun came up.

While Easy hammered outside in the shed, Myesha stayed busy inside Aunt Trulla's house. She cooked, watched over her aunt, and supervised Ezella Neptune and Sidney Jr. She paid little attention to Aunt Trulla's stained glass puzzle or *that man outside hammering lie a fool.* It took Ezella Neptune to thaw the ice between her father and Myesha. When she read the child crawled into her lap. Sidney Jr. was more interested in the stained glass his great aunt slid around the table. Myesha read aloud and sung. Ezella Neptune sang along. Their voices flowed out the window, into the yard, and into the shed where Easy worked. He'd stop and listen before continuing to work. She looked up one day at Easy standing in the kitchen doorway watching her.

"I think your father needs you," she said to Ezella Neptune and started to put her out of her lap.

"No. She's fine. She needs that kind of love in her life," Easy said. He got a drink of water and went back outside.

Myesha sung a while longer and stopped. She rested her chin in Ezella Neptune's hair and prayed silently. Aunt Trulla looked at her.

"Oh Lord," Aunt Trulla said and went back to playing with the stained glass. "The man who broke this glass had a storm in his head. The man out yonder got a storm in his heart. I feel the wind in my bones."

The window was the last item Easy installed. It was a few inches smaller that the hole, but he made it fit tight by framing boards around it and hammering them into the wall. He filled in small chinks with caulk. A heavy extension cord snaked through the yard from the house to the shed. Sunlight streamed through the window and the walls were tinted with colorful hues. The dove seemed to fly toward the skylight he cut into the roof.

Easy tricked Sidney into buying a futon and a bedside table to furnish the shed turned house, by telling him it was to be their love nest. The futon covered in red velvet and the stained glass added sacredness to the would-be love hideaway. Easy looked around the room at what he had created. His heart trembled and his knees buckled. He raised his hands and fell across the futon. Tears flowed and as he caressed the red velvet cloth he thought of Myesha.

One evening soon after he had mowed the lawn, Easy showered and put on clean clothes. Myesha set his place at the dinner table, but instead of sitting down to eat, he grabbed his plate and mumbled something about eating in his new home. Myesha shrugged and sat down to eat.

"Aunt Myesha I made an A on my math test," Sidney Jr. said proudly.

"I made a A plus," Ezella Neptune countered. "And I got a ribbon for my drawing."

"What did you draw," Myesha asked.

"I drawed..."

"Drew," Myesha corrected.

"I drew a church with a pretty glass window. Just like in my daddy's house."

Myesha smiled. She looked at the space between Ezella Neptune and Aunt Trulla and felt unsettled by the empty chair. She and Maura started in on the dishes when everyone had finished eating. She remembered a missing plate and started to send Maura after it. Instead, she gave her sister the dishtowel and went outside to the shed. Myesha walked in on Easy lying on the futon gazing at the stained-glass window. It was summer, and the sun streamed through the window. He got up and retrieved the plate from the table.

"My bad. I should have brought this back inside."

Myesha looked around the room at the bed, the leather recliner, the table and silver lamp, the red rug, and the stained-glass window.

"Would you like a tour of the castle?"

Myesha smiled. "It's very beautiful out here."

"It's lonely without a queen." Easy touched her arm.

She moved to the side. However, she didn't jerk her arm away.

"I'm sure it won't be lonely for long. There are many women without husbands walking around these streets."

"And your husband?" Easy asked looking at Myesha.

"I'm married to my work for the Lord. Besides aren't you and Sidney married to my sister?" Myesha smiled before turning to go back inside Aunt Trulla's. Easy stared through the transparent part of the window as Myesha carried the plate clutched to her bosom.

"That Neptune bitch," he said to himself.

That night Myesha had vivid dreams. She dreamed of men chasing her and holding her down. She felt them mount her and cover her face with their gritty hands. She dreamed she looked in the sky and saw an entire city on the horizon on fire. The dreams the disturbed her, but the one that made her heart race was her dream of Easy driving his car too fast and going over a cliff and bursting into flames.

As the days went on, Aunt Trulla and the children got on her nerves more than usual, and she was cross. She said very little to Maura and slept at the very edge of the king size bed. She tried one night to draw Maura into a conversation about Easy, but Maura clammed up. But Myesha was restless and wanted to know things about the dark man who had poured his seed into her sister.

The two women lay in silence in the huge round room. In another part of the house, Sidney Jr. whimpered from a bad dream and Aunt Trulla comforted him. Sidney slept on the couch. They heard him turn and fart.

"You bring up Easy because you hate me and want to rub dirt in my face," Maura said quietly.

A siren wailed in the distance. A twig snapped near the window. In a moment a stream of water splattered the leaves. The water stopped, and the women knew Easy was standing near the window shaking the last drop of piss from his dick. They heard the grass crunching under his bare feet as he made his way back to the shed. Myesha spoke when the shed's door slammed.

"I was in Liberia when the National Liberation Front cut through the country, raping and slaughtering thousands. I was beaten. A young nun from the Order of St. Cecile got caught in regular civilian clothes. After the soldiers raped her and tore her open down below, they cut off her arms and breasts. When we found her and brought her to the hospital, her last words she murmured was, 'Forgive them, Lord.' For what earthly reason would I have for hating you, Maura? I've seen so much in this world."

"You used to harbor grudges and wait for the right time to get even," Maura said.

"Perhaps then, yes. But Big Mama Mamie's beating purged me of that. I became numb to suffering. I lay in my twin bed in agony, but my soul got up and left. I knew I would not spend another night in this house. I don't remember anything about the next morning. I don't know what we ate for breakfast. I was just a shadow among shadows. When we parted in Vanguard's hallway, and I snuck out to that boy's car, I knew a new life awaited me. I gave Robert my virginity for a few bucks—not for love or that I thought he was cute. I gave it up for a practical reason."

"You was the devil, and I was a saint in Big Mama Mamie's eyes."

Myesha chuckled. "I used that devil when I wrapped my arms around Robert. He worked so hard taking what he thought was valuable and precious. Had he not been wearing a condom; I would have gotten pregnant for certain. I carried my numbness on the bus to New York, through the streets of Manhattan and, the killing fields of Liberia."

"Well, you've come full circle, sister. You're back in this house, this same room—though it's bigger, it's same room. Is your numbness wearing off? A man outside in that stained glass hut wants to know just how practical you are."

"He's your man, sister. You have his child."

"Is he my man or is he any woman's man? He's got wings on his back, and like a fly, he lights everywhere, even on another man." Maura asked bitterly. "So it's my turn to be numb. And sister..." Myesha turned to see Maura's face. "Why did you call Big Mama a hypocrite in your note you wrote when you ran away?" Myesha was silent. "You saw those photographs of her and the Deacon," Maura continued. "Her truth is our truth. We can't run and hide from that truth. We're a couple of whores." Myesha stretched her eyes. Maura turned over and pretended to be asleep.

Myesha was quiet as she mulled over Maura's pointed question and statement.

A few nights passed, and Myesha couldn't sleep. She sat on the porch under the yellow lamp bulb and glanced at passages from her bible. She read and reread Leviticus: "You shall not lie with a male as with a woman; it is an abomination."

However, her mind was far from the book. She tried to rein in her thoughts and bring them back to the Lord, but the heat of the night made her sweat. Myesha looked at the chinaberry tree, and her memories of the beating came back stark and clear as if it had just happened yesterday. Her numbness fell away. She winced as if she felt stinging welts on her thighs and buttocks. She thought a glass of water would cool her off and slipped into the kitchen and filled two glasses. She didn't bother to throw a robe over her thin muslin gown. Myesha tiptoed past the snoring Sidney and went out into the yard. She stood at the door of the shed and knocked softly. When there was no answer, she started to go back into the house but instead turned and twisted the doorknob. The door opened, and she stuck her head in just enough so she could jerk it out if there were another woman in bed with Easy. The stained-glass window lets in a sliver of light and Myesha saw that Easy was alone in the bed. He sensed her presence and woke up.

"I thought, I thought you might want some water." Myesha held the glass toward Easy. He started to swing his body over the bed to reach for the water, but he realized he was naked under the sheets. He held out his hand, and Myesha stretched as if reaching over a fence and gave him the glass.

"Thank you," Easy said and took a drink. He paused and looked up at the dark silhouette of Myesha in the doorway. A light shined on her, and her whole body was outlined in the thin muslin. This time there was no switch to turn off any light. He finished drinking and moved over to make a place for her to sit on the bed. She thought for a moment and stood beside the bed. He looked thin and harmless under the velour bedspread. She sat down and smiled at him. He smiled back at her. In a moment he reached up and put his hand on her shoulder.

"What kind of man are you who—" Myesha's tongue-lashing stopped in mid-sentence when Easy pulled her down to the bed and wrapped his arms around her. She did not resist.

The next day, when Easy came up behind Myesha in the kitchen stirring a pot of peas and put his hands on her shoulders, she turned around and slapped his face.

"I'm not a whore like Maura," she yelled and ran out of the room.

Easy stood and rubbed his jaw. All they had done last night was kiss. He had wanted to go further, but he rolled off when she objected. And yet she slapped him. Easy wondered if she slapped him for respecting her. "A bitch don't mean nothing she say," Plank used to tell him. Easy picked up the spoon Myesha had dropped.

Myesha flung herself across the bed, threw off her scarf, and cried. The Lord had been her strength throughout her years in Africa. He had shielded her from harm and even if harm came her way, he made her numb so she could endure without feeling. The Lord had numbed her that time in the Congo when a UN Peacekeeper soldier grabbed her arm.

He had come into the tent where she was tending the victims of the rebel forces. She felt his eyes on her as she moved amongst the cots. He cleared his throat, and she turned around. His face was the color of ink. She barely could see the whites in his eyes peering from beneath his helmet. The tent was stifling, and her robe clung to her ass and thighs as if she was wearing pantaloons. She saw him grab his crotch, but a message came over his walkie-talkie and distracted him. By the time Myesha passed him with a pail of dirty water, his attention had returned to her. He grabbed her arm and kissed her, and for a moment his lips made her tremble. But before her knees buckled, the Lord stepped in, and she jerked away and grabbed a handful of dirty syringes to defend herself. The soldier gave her a hateful look before slinking out of the tent. But that night as she lay on her cot Myesha thought about that kiss. She asked the Lord to take away the tremble in her body, but he refused and let the devil take control of her hands and with her hands between her legs, the devil had his way with her.

"And here comes another devil," Myesha said picking her scarf off the floor. As she smoothed her robe, she stopped for a moment and felt her belly. Yes she had let Easy kiss her, and he was naked when he rolled briefly on top of her, but he stopped when she protested. "Most certainly not," Myesha said to herself in the mirror.

My Manhood Is Very Important to Me

I believe this, you can be a punk, but you just have to keep that punk shit on the downlow, you know what I'm saying? You know, don't be actin' all faggish and shit—wearing lipstick, wigs, and that eye shadow bullshit. You need to hard up you know, uncross your legs pull your crotch up like I do. You see a nigga know I'm a hard motherfucker the way I pack my shit. Even you, if you had on some men clothes you could pull your dick up too. But wearing a leather skirt like you some kind of bitch—what kind of shit is that? You got legs and thighs bigger than mine, and I know I'm a man. I just like a nigga sometime—you know, just to kick it with. Get our nut together and not have any of that psychological warfare that bitches can put a dog through—you know what I'm sayin? And with another nigga you ain't got to worry about no "accident" that's going to stay in your pocket for twenty-years or some shit like that. Yeah, I likes a hard nigga like me.

Skate and me used to kick it until some motherfucker iced him over some bad shit that Skate sold him. Yeah, me and Skate was tight. His ol' lady leave the house to go to her slave, thirty minutes later I'm over at Skate's fucking him. And he could suck my dick like a motherfucker. I'd nut all over the place. I'd do him right too. I ain't scared to eat me a piece of ass long as it's clean. A tongue ain't just for talkin' you know. After we had exhausted ourselves beyond our limits and possibilities, we'd lay there and let the cum dry and the cool breeze blow over our asses and shoot the shit about this and that. We mostly talked about our bitches. You know by me and Skate having each other, we could deal with our bitches better. When a bitch gets on the rag and don't want to give you no pussy?—well that's okay 'cause your boy will take care of you. 'Course you wouldn't know nothing about that shit. You almost a bitch yourself. You know, I kind of thought you was a bitch at first. Then when I looked closer at your face and saw them razor bumps, I said to myself, "Damn, Avery, that's a punk." My whores call me Avery 'cause I'm a very good nigga to my whores—you know what I'm saying? You kind of look like Skate a little bit. Got them big soft plum looking lips like him. Yeah, I loved them lips. Skate kind of favored my pops. I used to wonder sometimes if Skate was maybe a blood brother.

Skate and me was beginning to have some static between us. He started hanging round other punks, you know what I'm saying—getting into that gay lifestyle shit, going to punk bars, and shit like that. I told Skate I wasn't going to no punk bar. Punk bars ain't got nothin in 'em but punks that look like you... Well, you know what I'm saying. I'm not tryin' to call you out, and yeah, I got my punk side, but I'm a hard straight-up nigga first. Ain't never goin' to catch me in no skirt. Then Skate started to want to hang too much. He started talkin' about us gettin' rid of our bitches and me and him livin' together. Skate was my boy, but I couldn't hang with all that punk shit living together like husband and wife. I loved him in a hard nigga kind of way. But I was a little relieved when he got iced. I mean I didn't want to have to ice him myself. How you goin' to ice somebody you love, I asked myself. Is it that much liquor in the world to get you drunk enough to ice somebody you love? But my manhood is very important to me. I got to keep the family going. Got to bring some little Avery's into this world. Can't let all of my seeds dry up on sheets and get flushed down toilets in the tips of condoms. That's why I can't hang with too much of that punk shit. What would my family say?

Now like I said to you (you with them Skate looking black plum lips) the other night when I gave you my cell phone number, I said we can kick it for a while. I got what you like, and you got what I like. Just don't try to put no hooks in me. You down with that?

A'ight then tell a man somethin.' Come over here and sit down next to me. I don't bite. Le's get you out of this wig and dress shit. Damn, you got some muscles. I could turn you into a hard nigga. I'm glad you ain't got on no female draws. But I do like to see a nigga in some red draws like you got on. They makin' your ass look round and tight. I like my niggas to have round bubble asses. I like an ass like that on a bitch too. But it's hard to find a bitch that let you fuck her in the ass. And why should they? They got what God gave them for fuckin.' 'Yeah, take off my shirt if you want to. Shit yeah, I work out. A motherfucker got to stay hard unless he wants to get jacked all the time. Skate and me used to work out together by liftin' old cinder blocks from the tore down funeral home. I heard Doc Preacher say you get your strength from the dead. Them cinder blocks made me a strong motherfucker.

Ouch! Don't pinch my nipples so hard with them damn nails. Your nails ruin my illusions. I want you to be a man, not a bitch. Just play with me with your fingertips. Yeah, rub my stomach. I know it's round. It's round 'cause it's full of sweet potato pie. You see I ate my girl Charlene the other night. Hell no I ain't goin' to tell you nothin' about Charlene. You might hard up and go try to get a piece of the sweet potato pie for yourself. Charlene's got a soft spot for punks. Always tellin' me I ought to be more sensitive. Ain't that some shit?

Yeah, slip off your draws. Take 'em off real slow. Aw shit, man, you packin.' You a punk and almost twice as big as me. Put your arms around me. Yeah, baby, that feels good. I like the way I feel in your arms. I want some tongue too. Them lips feel good. Don't put no hickey on me, dog. I don't want no static from Charlene. I got somethin' for you too. You like my dick? Then swallow me, nigga! Tha's right all down your throat. I want to feel my dick through your throat. Sweet Jesus! Goddamn, Andrea! Wait. Hold up. Hold up. I can't hang with that Andrea shit. I'm goin' to call you Dre.' I likes to call a dog's name when he's sucking my dick. Yeah, Dre' that's the way I like it. That feels good. You suck dick better than Skate. Wait, man. I ain't ready to nut yet. Look a here. Why don't you do me a favor and put your wig back on and put your draws back on. Okay now walk around the room. Walk real slow and sexy like. Yeah, I like that. Wiggle that ass a little bit. Ooh shit! Hell, you look more sexy than Charlene. Hell yeah!

Hey stop! What the hell you think you doin'? Don't put that wig on me. Take that shit off me. I ain't no bitch, Motherfucker! I'm a straight up hard nigga. I'll kill a motherfucker tryin' to steal my manhood. You understand? A'ight then. Shit. Puttin' a goddamn wig on me. My mama tried that shit once. Call herself go in' to punish my ass by makin' me wear one of her wigs 'round the house. I fixed her. I cut up every damn wig she owned. Yeah, she beat my ass, but in the end I won. She didn't try that shit no more. You don't fuck with a nigga's manhood. My pops wasn't around that much, but I know by instinct, that a nigga got to protect his manhood from bitch's and punk ass white boys. You think I'm gonna let you put some white girl lookin' wig on me? Hell no, mother fucker! Okay you sorry. Just let me chill a little bit.

I'm a'ight now. Come back over here next to me. Open your mouth, Dre' and let me give you another little taste of Mr. Avery. And you know what? My tongue is twitchin', dog. I want some of your sweet potato pie tonight.

MINISTER Q

"*The white man is a filthy beast! I said the white man is a filthy beast! His mind is rotten with carnal cancer and bloodlust. The genocide he wreaks on this earth and his pornographic industries are evidence of his cancer raging out of control. This cancer, my Brothers, and Sisters, is killing Allah's children!*

The white man's carnal images in the media fuel the filthy lyrics rappers and so-called poets spew out over our airwaves. This carnality is a vicious Satan running rampant, causing homosexuality and AIDS to invade our communities, and decimating our people. The white man is a sick sick soul!"

Little brown Sister Gloria trembled and rocked, awed by the virile velocity of Minister Q as he sprayed his words like machine gun fire over the assembly. Minister Q, the "Apostle" of the "New Nation," a spin-off from the old Nation of Islam, had a "Message for America" this morning. His epistles burst from the bulging veins in his neck and shot from his tongue like venomous bullets. His congregation craned their necks to catch every drop, but no one was thirstier than Sister Gloria. She absorbed every drop of sweat trickling from Minster Q's forehead, every bead soaking his white shirt and exposing the deep muscles of his chest. Sweat soaked the waistline of Minister Q's black trousers. She imagined the oily dew making his buttocks shine like onyx. She closed her eyes and inhaled the musk of his dangling sex deeply. Her lips parted.

Sister Gloria's eyes popped open, and she jammed her fists into her lap. She was a pure and saved sister now. However, she couldn't drive away the funkiness of her past life—the funk of men's unwashed bodies, dollars that reeked of cigarette smoke and sweat, and stale gin on thick lips. These odors lingered in Sister Gloria's nostrils like the stench of unwashed panties. And here the young minister was ranting against the very thing poisoning Sister Gloria's thoughts this morning: Lust and filth! She closed her eyes, but instead of her lascivious thoughts vanishing, Minister Q stood in front of her black, naked, and erect. She started to weep. A Sister seated next to her offered a tissue. The congregation assumed Sister Gloria was overcome by the message instead of the messenger.

You think listening to Billy Graham is going to save ex-crackheads like you? Hell no! That white man isn't wasting his spit on you. His Jesus—a white limp-haired facsimile of Allah—that he lies and says loves you, was created by white devils for white devils to glorify themselves and to conquer dark races. And you Baptist jigaboos and Methodist jigaboos, foolishly quiver at the feet of this blue-eyed icon on Sunday. You are fools for Satan.

But I too was once a fool. I was lost before I found Allah. I have been praying for black people since I was twelve before I knew the thing between my legs defined me as a man. Unlike our great brother Malcolm, I did not spend my youth chasing whores and glittery temptations. My blood is not tainted with drugs. I am not ashamed to say that the only woman who has seen me naked has been my grandmother who raised me from a baby.

The minister's words weaved through Sister Gloria's daydream of a smooth-skinned black boy on his knees with hands clasped in prayer. His dark eyelashes swept heaven as he implored God to save his people. She imagined herself, stripping out of her veil, robe, and underwear. She danced and waved her panties in the boy's face. Bowing low, she brushed her nipples across his thick lips, raised him from his knees and stripped him out of his clothes. Tears streamed down the boy's face. He smelled sweetly of violet scented soap and grape bubble gum. He rose and floated in midair. Taking, her hand, they floated toward Heaven in a heart-shaped cloud.

Sister Gloria shook her head as if she could shake these thoughts to the floor and mash them with her foot. How dare she sit in the front row of the women's section in Mosque #8 in her pure white veil while muck swirled in her head? She thought she sniffed the odor of rotten cabbage seeping from her body. She clenched her thighs closer together and jammed her hands into her lap to keep other sisters from picking up this scent. If only her father were alive to rebuke her and put his fist upside her head, thought Sister Gloria. She couldn't remember the man ever setting foot in a church or a mosque, but he could rebuke like any preacher when his liquor turned his eyes red.

A freaky john might cure her of her iniquity, Sister Gloria thought—the kind of man who used a belt or cigarette butt on a woman. But she wasn't a prostitute anymore. That was the past. Maybe if she confessed to Minister Q, her filthy desire for him to kiss the secret places on her body and for her lips to touch the secrets of his body, perhaps Minister Q would become so enraged he would beat her himself and put her back in a righteous place. She had to have a private meeting with the Minister. But how?

The young minister always arrived at Mosque #8 in the back of a black Mercedes-Benz thick with the bodies of his guards. Another car followed. His men surrounded him and hustled him straight to the podium from which he spoke and afterward, they hustled him away. For security reasons, his address was a secret. Sister Gloria's work for the mosque was limited to vacuuming its carpets and cleaning its toilets. Minister Q did have an office at the mosque, but it was behind a maze of locked doors. She could not even get close to the kitchen where older women prepared Minister Q's meals. How would she ever get close to the Minister? Luck was certainly not her best friend.

For all of her life, fate had been unkind to small brown Gloria. Cruel luck stole her mother away soon after she was born. Her father drowned his sorrow with liquor and reefer. His hands itched and he constantly scratched them. When he hit "Little Glory," her entire body felt as if it were on fire. Unkind luck stole away the *nice white lady* who was teaching Little Glory how to cook, sew, and read

German—just popped up one day and squeezed the woman's heart as she and "Little Glory" were making biscuits.

Bad luck had made her pregnant five times. It blocked her escape from her cruel pimp until someone stuck him in his head with an ice pick. In her "clean days," unkind luck beat Sister Gloria out of good jobs and sent her to work flipping hamburgers at White Castles.

Sundays slipped by like pages in the Koran. Minister Q's angry "whitey" hating eyes blinded him to Sister Gloria's wide almond-colored loving eyes. She began to feel annoyed at Minister Q. How could he be so blind, she wondered. Why didn't he see her? She blamed it on the robes and veils. They hid everything Sister Gloria thought a man ought to see—thighs, shoulders, and breasts. Some women even hid their mouths and wore dark glasses to hide their eyes. But Sister Gloria did not hide her mouth and eyes. She wondered if her eyes alone could speak loud enough to the Minister's heart and stir up the jazz between his legs? Perhaps the fire roaring out of his mouth had consumed all of his music, she thought. Could it be that the Minister had sacrificed his jazz to Allah, and there was no hope for her? She knew that without music, a man could not be trapped by a woman's charms—he could not love a woman. Music was a man's blueprint for understanding a woman. She learned this from listening to her father's music.

Sister Gloria despaired. Her eyes drifted and lingered over the Minister's bodyguards. Perhaps they were not so "pure." She hoped they had allowed women to see them naked and had let their blues spin melodies between a woman's thighs. Sister Gloria caught in her sights a sand-colored guard. She imagined standing in the light of his amber eyes as sweet honey dripped over her lips and breasts, making her tingle all over. Weeks flowed lazily into red summer, and Minister Q turned into a dark shadow. Robert X had returned her gaze.

Her apartment was tiny. The living room window faced the backside of a warehouse. The small window of her bedroom was the only source of light. When the evening sun slipped through the cracks of the Venetian blinds, she saw dust particles swimming in the air and lighting on the furniture. Whenever she made a move to get out of bed to clean, dust, or cook, Robert X reached for her. He lay enchanted by the "charms" of Sister Gloria's street days. She knew the secret place on his body that made him tremble and moan like a sinner at an altar. Her bed was his temple and he worshiped there every evening while his wife worked.

One leg in the east
One leg in the West
and Robert in the middle
doing his best.

"I'll bet you're the only one of Minister's Guards who dares to sing the blues and play a guitar," She remarked after listening to Robert X's rendition of a blues melody.

The guitar was as secretive as their relationship. His wife would not allow the instrument in their home. He had to keep it at his mother's place.

"We've all had past lives, Sister. I keep a little bit of my history in my fingers."

"Your fingers have been enjoying the fruits of my past."

Robert X raised himself and leaned on his elbow. Veins traveled from his forearm and disappeared in his thick bicep. He watched Sister Gloria gazing at him. Her eyes were direct and unapologetic as she stroked his veins.

"I'm not about your past. I'm about your present," he said.

"Humph," she grunted and got up. She had been annoyed to find out he was married. She wanted the wholeness of a man. Not the furtive fumbling minutes in cars, cheap motels or alleyways. She had started to stop their affair, but then he was promoted to Lieutenant Guard in Minister's Q's guard detail. Though her lust for Minister Q had dimmed, his essence was like an eternal flame deep inside. Robert X fed her tidbits of meat that satisfied her gnawing hunger. And at least, she had hours with him—slow, languid hours that allowed the oils to pour out of their skin like nectar from flowers.

Sister Gloria returned to the bed with her mouth full of crushed ice. She spread and lifted his thighs. Her cold mouth took all of him in. His eyes rolled to the back of his head as if he were dying. He grasped the iron bedposts as if jolts of electricity were shooting through his body. Her tongue rolled all over his manhood, probed deep into his anus and that secret place underneath his testicles. Sweat flowed down his face. He grabbed the back of her head and thrust deep. He bellowed out her name three times. On the third time, Gloria swallowed deep all of his bitterness.

"You know a lot about men, Gloria Jean," Robert blurted out as she raised herself from between his legs and wiped her chin. She didn't like it when he called her that. His wife was named Jean and usually sat three chairs over from Sister Gloria. She sensed the fact that they sat so close to one another made the affair more exciting to him. She imagined him envisioning her, and his wife in the same bed on either side of him.

"So does the Minister have a past life?

"He's too young to have a past. He's only twenty-four."

This fact was news to Sister Gloria. His bearing and the ferociousness with which he delivered his message had made her think he was, at least, ten years older.

"He is the future of the New Nation," Robert X continued.

"The future has a past."

Robert X slapped her on her right cheek. "Stop trying to dig for dirt."

She grasped his hand and held it to her stinging face. She closed her eyes and for a moment as if it was the Minister's hand she was holding. She kissed his fingers.

"This is not the first time you've tried to sneak questions about him. Your interest in the Minister offends me," Robert scolded.

"I'm sorry, baby."

"I sometimes wonder whose dick you're really sucking."

Sister Gloria said nothing.

"But here is something about the man-boy, which might interest you. After services and on our way to his home, we have to stop at Game Depot so he can buy the latest Xbox Game. How's that for your man?"

"Robert, I've never had any desires for the Minister. I was only asking out of innocent curiosity."

"That's what got the cat killed. Get your mind off that boy and back to your man."

Sister Gloria snuggled up to Robert X and laid her head on his chest. She listened to his beating heart. He hummed a slow bluesy song until she fell asleep.

Six months later she visited his body lying in a gray casket at Small's Funeral Home far away from the Mosque. His wife Jean was nowhere in sight. Only his mother and a few other women sat and watched his corpse. Sister Gloria hid her eyes behind a pair of bug-eyed shades as she strode up to the coffin. The hem of her black trench coat brushed her knees. She touched him to see if any song beat from his heart. Her fingers caressed his drum-tight chest until someone cleared their throat.

Robert X's death had been a mysterious one. He was found in his car in a field with the motor running. His torn underwear was wound around his neck tight as a tourniquet and looped around the driver's side doorframe. His pants were found a few feet away from the car. The only clues the cops had were a few strands of blond hair balled in his fists. The cops said he most likely had been playing a dangerous game of asphyxiation with someone and it got out of hand. A month before he died, he spoke of quitting the Minister's Guard detail. He said a white man was following him, but he gave no other details. When Gloria pressed for more information, he balled up his fists.

A rumor floated through the air, about the time of his death, that he had stolen money from the Mosque. She wondered was that the reason the mosque had refused to hold his services. Or was it the strange circumstances of his death. Minister Q's only mention of Robert X came in a bitter statement he made from his pulpit.

"Satan sent a snake among the guards to bite us. But he was so vicious and vile he turned on himself before he could destroy any of Allah's people. God is greater than any white devil and any black Satan that walks this earth."

Jean sat and nodded her head stoically as the Minister spoke. Gloria wanted to strangle her. How could she let her husband be compared to a snake?

Luck

Sister Gloria didn't recognize luck right off. She was busy observing the guards, noting their unshaved and swarthy complexions. A few of them had a slick sheen to their skin. She imagined them clammy and cold to the touch. Their eyes darted back and forth into the crowd and amongst each other as if they each had a secret that might betray them any moment. "These are the snakes," Sister Gloria said to herself.

Luck flew like a speck in the corner of her eye. Minister Q's hands were flailing the pulpit as always, and his voice high and strained as he denounced the "great white Satan's of commerce." A scrap of paper flew from the minister's hand and landed on the dais between him and his wall of bodyguards. No one paid it any attention. They assumed the paper contained some filthy refuse from the Minister's body—perhaps his spit or his mucous. The flock wanted no part of that. They treasured the words that he spoke but not the waste that was as much a part of the Minister as his words. The crumpled napkin survived feet that kicked and crushed it. It survived high heels that dragged it and threatened to shred it to pieces. No one stopped to pick it up.

The next day Sister Gloria came to vacuum. She ran the noisy Hoover mindlessly over various scraps of paper, pebbles, and a copper penny that made a loud clattering noise. Gloria stopped and examined the vacuum. After she shook the coin out of the cleaner and she had up righted it, her eyes fell on the wadded napkin next to the dais. Sister Gloria remembered it flying from Minister Q's hand. She scooped it up and jammed it in her pocket.

On the bus and miles away from Mosque #8, she exhaled. No one had seen her picking up the paper. Questions would have been asked as to why she didn't put it in the trash. Or if she thought it was important enough to stuff in her pocket, why not alert a guard? Gloria studied the words written in a left-hand slant on the napkin. She read the napkin as if it were a chapter in the book of the Koran, instead of a note with a few simple words:

> Quincy,
> you Master Beckons
> Oasis rm 8A Ashland N clark tonight,
> Love—
> B.

At first, Sister Gloria panicked. She thought this was all some mosque business, and here she had stolen a note that would keep Minister Q from an important appointment. Now she really deserved a beating. And it ought to be done with fists and coat hangers (like her pimp used to do). As Sister Gloria read the note, other voices crept into her head—very prophetic voices whispering, "There's more to this, there's more to this." She felt jittery. The lurching bus made her stomach queasy.

Sister Gloria kept her eyes on the napkin as if it were money. She didn't care whether the token held dried sperm or spit within its folds. She didn't know much about DNA, but she knew the workings of conjure women like her aunt who lived deep in the swamps of Louisiana. All her Aunt Day needed was a little bit of spit, shit, or hair to make somebody love you, to make your enemy twist in agony on their deathbed, or to make your baby look like the man you wished was its father. Sister Gloria fell in love with the crumpled and abused piece of paper and poured over the words daily.

Master? There was no title of master in the ministerial hierarchy. Brother, Minister, Prophet, and even Apostle, but Master? And that "you" instead of "your." The ministers were college-educated. How could one of them make such a mistake? Why would they rendezvous in an out of the way motel? The Oasis was a miserable place hunched down between the freeway and Wrigley Field. The yellowish walls of its rooms were spotted with sperm and dried blood. Sister Gloria knew it well. It had been her stomping ground when she picked up tricks.

"Quincy love B," Sister Gloria chanted to herself as she washed her snow-white veil. When it was dry, she hung it in the closet next to her dead father's old suits. She took out her red thigh-high leather skirt and a white midriff blouse with tattered fringes. Her long blond wig cascaded over her shoulders like a gold scarf. She remembered her father's old twenty-two pistol. She hadn't been out on the cuts in a while and felt she should take more than Allah with her as the gun nestled in her bosom.

"Quincy love B," she sang over and over in her head as she rode the bus toward the Oasis.

The fetid night air lapped at Sister Gloria's thighs like hot stale breath. Men eyed her legs, from her knotty calves to her slender thighs as she walked along the sidewalk. The warm wind beneath her skirt teased her and stirred up the urge to talk jive and bargain pieces of herself to the solitary men circling her in their cars. But Sister Gloria remembered her faith in Allah. She had confidence in some wild hope that luck would once again find her and put her in the hands of the Minister. Perhaps when he finished with this private Brotherhood business at the Oasis, he would take her in his strong arms, pull her into his temple, and lead her to secret places where his warm blood flowed. This place is where Sister Gloria yearned to go. She knew the ways of white men. Knew them better than Minister Q could ever know. She knew them when they shed their clothes, exposed their hot pink bodies and called her "mama" and "goddess," and sipped her piss. She knew them when they called her "nigger bitch" and thrust their pricks down her throat. Minister Q couldn't tell her a damned thing about white men. But he could let her have entry into his temple to savor his sweet fruits.

It was this desire that made Sister Gloria walk in her high heeled and thin-soled shoes over the glass and pebble-strewn parking lot of the Oasis. She walked to the back lot of the motel where cars looking sheepish and guilty waited. The Minister's Black Mercedes stood out proud and arrogant from the herd of small sedans. Its polished grill and big shiny headlights were brazened and haughty. Sister Gloria touched the car and stared up at the dull lights that shined from a few windows of the Oasis. She looked for silhouettes of men hunched over tables or pacing the floor. She searched for a door guarded by lean men in bow ties. Sister Gloria saw nothing that gave evidence of any meeting in the cube-like rooms of the Oasis.

Eight-A was in a little alcove facing a wall. There were no rooms to either side, and it was not near the main stairwell. The alcove was unlighted. Sister Gloria peered through the tiny glass peephole into the dimly lit room. A dark unclothed shadow rubbed a towel over its legs and thighs. She knew it was Minister Q. She blinked her eye and a ghostlike figure appeared and hovered near the Minister. The ghost's yellow hair shined under the room's ceiling bulb. Sister Gloria watched, and the "ghost" disappeared into what she assumed was the bathroom. Minister Q lay on his belly. He looked toward the door and pulled a sheet over his buttocks as if he sensed a presence at the peephole. Sister Gloria looked away for a moment. In those few seconds, Minister Q turned off the light. Darkness greeted her when she turned to gaze into the room. Alarmed, she started to knock, but quickly realized the futility of it. The Minister was obviously occupied. What could she do, Sister Gloria wondered? Ask to join him and his blond-haired trick?

A white woman? A white devil? Sister Gloria's anger rose from the pit of her stomach and settled on the back of her throat. "I knew he was lying about all of that only grandma has seen him naked stuff," Sister Gloria said to herself. She tried to ease her mind by relegating the woman to the aimless ways men passed the time. The woman swirled in the muck of liquor, gambling, and porn. "*It's not the liquor I love, baby. It's the right it makes me feel,*" Sister Gloria remembered her father saying. The woman was no doubt just a tool the minister was using perhaps in a moment of boredom. But why a white woman? Why not her, she asked herself. Gloria dropped her arm to her side and turned from the peephole. Her body pressed against the hard door. Her stomach tingled. Her thighs caressed the rough surface of the door. She thought of course, hairy legs brushing up against her. Moans began to seep through the door like music. She stood mesmerized by the sonorous sighs, wishing her nipples were the fruit that the minister was kissing and gnawing. Her legs and lips parted. Sister Gloria closed her eyes and imagined the minister's black hands and rough lips seeking the sweet meat of her body.

Suddenly, "Nigger!"

She opened her eyes and wondered who had uttered the shrill nasally vibrato. She looked around. There was no one in the stairs and walkways.

"Nigger!" the voice shouted again. This time, the harshness was tempered with a hint of melodic sweetness. Sister Gloria realized the cry was coming from behind door 8A. It was Southern and masculine. It raked her spine and she froze. She thought of Lot's wife and wondered if she had turned into a pillar of salt.

"Nigger!" the voice twanged louder. Mingled with the twang, was Minister Q's plaintive urgent bleating.

"Please, Master, please. Please, Master, don't whip me. I'm one of your good niggers, Master. Ooh, Master! Please don't whip me. I can be good."

The voice of the "slave master" answered, "Shut up, nigger! Bring your sweet black ass back over here and tell me how sorry you are for disobeying me."

"I'm sorry, Master. I'm sorry I been a bad nigger boy, Master. If I promise to be good, Master, will you love me? Will you love me, Master, if I be good? Please, Master?"

Sister Gloria listened to the sharp slaps of hands against bare flesh. She heard shrieks and then the high and low cries that dissolved into "Master" cooing, "My sweet, sweet black nigger. Oh, my sweet, sweet nigger."

Thick mucus collected in her throat. She clamped her hand over her mouth and ran away from the door.

*T*he white man is the beast of the earth. Even his children are blood sucking vermin indoctrinated before they leave their mother's bloody womb that they are the masters of the dark races, the earth, the moon and stars of the heavens. But their so-called right of ownership is, in reality, a curse that damns them to hell. The conqueror spills oceans of innocent blood to be a conqueror. I stand here today and tell you the day is coming for the WHITE MAN to drown in the blood he has caused to spill. Allah *will not rest until every white devil is swallowed up and erased from the earth. The day is coming, I tell you.*

Dark shades hid Sister Gloria's eyes as she sat in her usual front row seat on the women's side of Mosque #8. She wondered if she was going blind. She tried to focus, but the minister and his guards faded to a milky haze. His once broad shoulders slumped forward and his skin appeared powdery and ashy. Salty sweat popped from his forehead and stung his eyes. He blinked and rubbed them frequently. The listeners around Sister Gloria fervently nodded at the Minister's words. But Sister Gloria was as still as a cat eying a bird. And like a cat observes its prey, so does a camera's lens hold onto the image caught in its large glass eye.

The glass eye was a digital camera she bought at a pawnshop. A young coworker at White Castles taught her how to download video and still images onto a tiny stick the size of one of her babies she had aborted. She kept this stick on a chain close to her heart.

She wore her new "dignity" like a comfortable old sweater. Voices at the mosque whispered about the "new" serene, dignified sister—though Sister Gloria had been coming there for months. Someone pointed her out to Minister Q. He glanced curiously as if he thought he remembered her from somewhere but said nothing. Sister Gloria, in turn, vacuumed without running into furniture and dusted without breaking things. Her glasses and veil hid the ocean of discontent that swirled behind her eyes. For weeks, the sound of water churned and roared in her head. She wished there was a river close by in whose waters she could toss her pain. She imagined wrapping her heart in her veil, stepping into the river, and letting her hurt float away.

As the red summer days turned to orange autumn, the roaring river in her head subsided. She stopped going to the Oasis and standing in front of unit of 8A. Sister Gloria locked away the memory stick full of photos and film of the Minister's car; the Minister in the fake mustache, t-shirt, and yellow warm-up pants; the Minister in blond wigs and dark shades. Sister Gloria ceased playing the tape of moans that had seeped through the door of 8A. She forgot about the minister lurking in dark out-of-the-way bars, drinking with and hanging on the arms of "B," brushing his hands through his hair, and catching the loose strands floating to the floor. She herself raked her fingers through Billy's hair one night in a tiny bar called the Blue Moon. Minister Q stared at her until she said in her deepest voice, "Baby, I don't want your man. But I do love this mop of curls on his head." All of that stuff, including the blond hair she had accumulated with her fingers while pretending to be a man who pretended to be a woman, she put in her father's old trunk. This change in her came after a handshake.

Sister Gloria was finishing up dusting the hallway near the Minister's office. The evening sun was falling, and a dull red haze colored the sky and slipped into the hall through the Venetian blinds. A door opened, and the Minister walked out of his office. Sister Gloria was startled by his presence. She had assumed he was not in the mosque that day because she did not see his car parked at the rear and there were no guards. The Minister walked toward the window and leaned heavily on the ledge and peered out. He sighed long and hard before he realized he wasn't alone. He turned and looked at Sister Gloria, who stood in the maroon shadows.

"How are you today, My Sister?" The Minister's voice was soft. Sister Gloria was surprised at how small and boyish his feet looked as he stood close to her. She could only see his feet because she kept her head slightly bowed, as it was the custom of Sisters at the mosque to do when they encountered a man with whom they weren't familiar.

"Fine, Minister, and you?" She asked as her eyes swept the floor. She thought about discarding that custom, raising her head, and meeting his eyes. But a voice told her if she raised her head all of the hurt inside her would rise also. And she might dig her nails into his face.

"I'm troubled, Sister," Minister Q, answered, "The sickness of this world is seeping into me."

Sister Gloria's heart stopped. She blurted out, "Minister, let me..."

The Minister cut her off. "Please pray for me, my serene Sister. Pray for me." He touched her hand, turned, and walked back into his office. The lock clicked softly in Sister Gloria's ears.

The mosque lit up. The haze disappeared from Sister Gloria's eyes. Her vision of Minister Q changed. She saw him like a wife sees her husband for the first time when the man has moved beyond sexy exotic love making machine—when he becomes a creature with warts. These warts might be his simple pettiness or childishness. Sometimes the warts are his infidelities and strange perversions followed by tears of sorrow and professions of love. The wife must decide to either love this "real" man or flee. Sister Gloria chose to love Minister Q. How could she belittle the Minister's lust for love and pain, she asked herself. She knew the search for love could take one to the depths of iniquity. If love landed you a stinging slap from a man's rough hands or his foot in your backside, at least, it was something. And if the Minister had to have his own special "something" then so it is. Who was she to judge, Sister Gloria asked. She would be much more loyal than Robert X's Jean and stand by Minister Q even to the end.

This love, under the iron gray winter Chicago Sky, took her high into vaporous white summer clouds. The seed of love grew in Gloria's heart, nourished by the fact that only she knew the Minister's dark side. Not only did she know the secret, but she also felt she knew why the enigma existed at all. Sister Gloria knew what it was like to carry burdens. She had toted her share—her mother's death, a drunken father, pimps, and her babies spilled into stainless steel bowls. The fact that only she knew the Minister's private life, Sister Gloria thought made her more intimate with the Minister. It was an intimacy no other simple woman at the mosque could ever have. She was the head wife. No other woman would ever have that position. She vowed to stand by the Minister's side, even the side that was full of the warts of his exotic sexuality. Sister Gloria would be there as he delicately and painfully walked the tightrope of his conscience stretched over a roaring fire. She would even accept "*B*" as some aberration. Though Sister Gloria had never married, she knew a good wife does what she can to keep her husband from falling. Sister Gloria had a startling image of the "good wife" in her head.

As a girl, Watergate meant little to her, except that the TV was full of jowly old men questioning people, snorting, and reading from a bunch of papers. But Gloria remembered one scene—the ghostlike white woman with her hair pulled tightly in a blond bun, sitting quietly and steely behind her man in horn-rimmed glasses. The man was getting grilled by "old farts" trying to throw him in the fire," is how her father had put it. Sister Gloria would do more for the Minister. She would walk with him across the tightrope as he deceived the people. She too would deceive so she could love her "husband" even better. Sister Gloria began to wear her short skirts and midriff exposing blouses under her robes. Her long blond wig was tucked securely underneath her veil and scarf.

As with all love and lovers, there were moments of doubt in Sister Gloria's heart. To strengthen her love, she took to the pitted streets and broken avenues around The Oasis. She sought young drunken college boys, baited and coaxed them into beating her by calling them names and making fun of their dicks. When a beating wasn't enough, she dared them to ram bottles into her. If the excruciating pain that made her scream and see blue lights wasn't enough to steel her resolve, she went home and whipped herself across the back with her father's old belts. "If the Lord could sacrifice himself why can 't I," Sister Gloria asked herself.

Sister Gloria was prepared to live out the rest of her life in this role of wounded wife until Brother Messenger mounted the podium one Sunday, and barely peering over it, spoke in a loud commanding voice: "The Honorable Minister Q and the Honorable Sister Aisha will be joined in a holy union by Minister F1 two weeks from today. May Allah bless and make this union fruitful for the New Nation."

The congregation applauded. At the urging of Minister Q, Sister Aisha stood and took a quick bow. She had covered herself from head to toe with a long veil. She hid her mouth and wore dark shades. When she sat down, Minister Q spoke:

One night Allah came and talked to me in my sleep. I saw him shrouded in the purple robes of the almighty, and his voice was as soft and distinct as a flowing river. When I awoke, it was revealed in my heart that I had been neglecting one of the black man's most important duties. Allah teaches us to respect the female for she manifests Allah's gentle spirit. From her womb come many fruits. Black men, it is our duty to protect these fruit bearers from the clutches of the great white Satan. He has many trinkets to lure the fruit bearers, and he will lure them from us and spoil them with his bad seed. Our mosque is full of fruit bearers that we black men, and only black men should cultivate—Sister Eugenia, Sister Gloria, Sister Tamara...

Sister Gloria stared at Minister Q. How dare he call her name and put her in the class of ordinary breeding machines, she thought to herself. I am your wife! I've gone to the hidden places where your wounds fester and stink like shit. I accepted you and walked with you in your despair. I sucked the pricks of white men because you did. I whipped my ass because he whipped yours. How can you toss me away like a spoiled apple for your Guards and other Ministers to slobber over?

Sister Gloria wept softly. Through her tears, she could see the Minister speaking, but did not hear him. There was a roaring in her head as if she was standing by the side of a highway. The Minister sunk closer to the floor and was soon on all fours. He began to bark like a hound. A horn sprouted from his head. Those around Sister Gloria applauded and urged the Minister on in his speech. The beast crept toward her. She felt its hot breath around her ankles. It caught the ends of her long veil in its teeth and tugged. Sister Gloria's scarf felt tight around her head. It squeezed her temples, and she stood up.

Startled by the sudden movement, Minister Q's guards bunched together quickly. They put one foot forward as if preparing to tackle her in case she ran toward the minister. A few sneaked their hands into their double-breasted coats and clutched cold steel. As Sister Gloria took a few steps from her chair, Minister Q's sermon faded like a song dying on the radio. The guards pressed their shoulders together and made a wall of human flesh between Sister Gloria and Minister Q.

Tears trickled down her cheek. With one hand she tore the veil from her head. Blond hair fell over her shoulders. The crowd murmured and looked at one another. With the same hand, Sister Gloria loosened a button on her robe. It slipped off and exposed her shoulders. The short red skirt and halter-top scantly covered her ass and bosom. The memory stick in her cleavage glinted under the mosque's lights. The crowd gasped and covered their mouths. Sister Gloria held out her hands. A guard took off his jacket and ran towards her. She held him at bay with her palm.

"Beat me, Jesus. Beat me, Master! Oh, master, beat me good! Jesus! Jesus! Jesus, beat me. Beat this flesh until it's soft and bloody. Master, I yield to your whip. Please, Master, whip this nigger until she shits!"

Sister Gloria spoke directly to Minister Q, who stared slack jawed. As she turned and started for the door, Minister Q saw what had made his followers gasp. Sister Gloria's back was crisscrossed with bright red stripes that ran from her shoulder blades to her lower back. She walked with her hands above her head through the dim mosque and into the cold blue day.

Minister Q's voice was cracked and strained as he tried to dismiss Sister Gloria's outburst as a product of the "great white Satan," but he choked on his words and lost his voice for the rest of the afternoon. In fact, he lost his voice forever at Mosque #8.

After Sister Gloria arrived home and changed into a black dress and veil, she mailed a package containing the memory stick to the minister of the rival Mosque #2. Enclosed also was a letter chronicling everything she had seen and heard at the Oasis. She sent another package to the police. It contained the note written on the napkin, along with strands of *B*'s blond hair. She wrote another note outlining her suspicions about the Robert X case.

The following Saturday night the police found Minister Q and "*B*" in room 8A. The frayed end of a whip was wound tight around the minister's neck. The handle was rammed into his anus. Minister Q lay prostrate on the floor caked in blood, piss, and shit. His feet were jammed into a pair of red stilettos. "*B*" lay on the bed clutching a small twenty-two-caliber pistol in his left hand. Blood seeped from the bullet hole in his heart.

Sister Gloria in Her Own Voice

"*The white man is a filthy beast! I said the white man is a filthy beast! His mind is rotten with carnal cancer and bloodlust. The genocide he wreaks on this earth and his pornographic industries are evidence of his cancer raging out of control. This cancer, my brothers and Sisters, is killing Allah's children!*

The white man's carnal images in the media fuel the filthy lyrics rappers and so-called poets spew out over our airwaves. This carnality is a vicious Satan running rampant, causing homosexuality and AIDS to invade our communities, and decimating our people. The white man is a sick sick soul!"

M*aybe if I confessed to the Minister directly, he would beat me himself. But I don't know if he's that kind of man. What kind of experience he have with women if ain't none seen him naked? He in his twenties and ain't no woman seen him naked but his grandma? Something ain't right with that picture. How is little ol' me ever to find out about this man if I can't even get close to him? He comes to the Mosque in that big black car that looks like a block of granite. Got burly guards on each side of him looking like bulls in suits. My job around here is to vacuum the rugs—all of them except in the Minister's office. I got to get promoted to do that. And it'll be twenty years before I'm even thought to be good enough to be allowed to join the women who cook his meals. Ain't enough luck in the world to get me close to that man.*

Well, there is plenty of luck in this world. It just doesn't land my way. Never have. I get the unlucky luck—like the woman set on fire by her man and gets her face burned off and she got to look at herself in mirrors and shiny spoons the rest of her life. Everybody says she lucky to be alive. To me that's unlucky luck. That's the kind of luck that took my mama when I was born. Left me with a daddy who drowned his sorrows in alcohol and women. When he wasn't hitting me, his women were. His hands itched all the time and when he hit me, it felt like my whole body was on fire.

My unlucky luck took away the white woman who taught me what little I know about cooking and sewing. I can make a mean lasagna. Unlucky luck just popped up and squeezed her heart until she couldn't breathe no more. Fool me, stood there and watched as she slid to the floor shaking like leaves on a windy day before she was still. People ask me later why I didn't call an ambulance for Mrs. Carlotti. I hunched my shoulders. But the real reason I didn't call for help was because my hands was full of flour and if I had wiped them on my dress, I was scared my daddy was going to beat me.

Now crazy luck did get me away from Red my pimp. But she took a long time sending somebody to stab that nigga in the head. The fight that got Red killed come up over a carton of milk—not money, not women, not dope—but a damn carton of sweet milk. Red was a fanatic over them little red cartons of Borden's milk. He'd buy dozens at a time and line them up in his refrigerator like little soldiers. If you messed with them, you got an ass beating you wouldn't forget. Well, one day, Red's brother decided to drink one. He shifted the cartons around to keep Red from seeing one was missing. When Red come in, he saw the cartons messed up and knew one of the milks was missing. He looked at me and another whore named Stella. We slyly nodded our heads toward the couch where Red's brother was asleep and got out of the room. When the fight was over, Red was on the floor with a pearl handled knife sticking out of his eye and I was a free woman, crooked mouth and all. I believe some kind of luck is going to put me next to the Minister. Just don't know what kind and when.

These Sundays at the Mosque slip by like pages turning in the Koran. I'm getting more annoyed at Minister Q. Is he blind? Why can't he see I'm special? Are these robes and veils hiding the things a man ought to see on a woman—like thighs, shoulders, and breasts? Some of my sisters even wear dark glasses and hide their mouths. But I won't go that far. I want my eyes to stir up some jazz between the minister's legs, unless all that whitey-hating fire done burned up his jazz.

My eyes wander over to the guards perched around the minister like a flock of black-suited magpies. Maybe they ain't so pure. Maybe jazz plays between their thighs, in their bellies, and tight lips. Maybe they think about us women from time to time while clutching their pistols. Maybe they've let plenty of women see them naked and they've spun melodies between a woman's thighs. Robert X, the assistant captain of the guards, caught my eyes staring at him. He slipped me a note when his wife wasn't looking. It said:

Sister, be my oasis

I can read between the lines. I'm good with words. Any man needs an oasis from the troubles of this world.

OTHELLO JONES

"**O**thello Jones! Othello Jones, is that you?"

"It's me and my twin brother."

"Your twin brother?"

"Must be. You called my name twice."

"You don't have to be so rude. Especially the kid I taught eleventh grade English, and the kid I took to the clinic to clear up a bad case of clap."

"I don't hug men. It ain't been no hundred years since I seen you last. And besides, I wuz born rude. My Mama said I gave my middle finger to the Doctor who slapped my ass to life."

"You sure are full of yourself."

"If I ain't full of me, who's goin' to be?"

"But don't you think humility has its place?"

"Yeah, under the bottom of my two-hundred-dollar alligator blue-skinned patent leather shoes!"

"Oh."

"Is you humble?"

"Well yes. I'm not boastful at all."

"You just told a contradiction."

"Life is full of . . ."

"If a bastard is humble on the outside of hisself, he raging with hatred on the inside of hisself."

"Well, I don't know."

"Don't you want to dig my grave and fill it full of me?"

"What?"

"Wouldn't you like to kill me, man?"

"No."

"Liar! You're itching to end my existence on the planet.

"No. You're my ex-pupil. Why would I want to kill you?"

"Yeah, you would. I see it in your sideways glance at me. You don't like my shoes, my gold watch, my four-hundred-dollar Brooks Brothers European cut blue silk suit that shimmers like the blue sea in front of your pale gray eyes, my white John Henry shirt with real pearl buttons, my Oscar de la Renta tie. And to top it all off you would severely despise my red Calvin Klein silk lowrise drawers if you could see them! And I know you hate this clean-cut Mister Joe masterfully put on my head. It makes your own stuff look like a wet mop. You white, but you not nearly as pretty as I am."

"I don't care enough about any of that."

"Apathy is murder, man! That's the knife you want to stick in me."

"Stop trying to cross me up."

"You gettin' closer, man."

"Closer to what?"

"Closer to forgettin' how humble you is."

"Nothing can shake me."

"Your Mama!"

"My Mother, what?"

"When this city was a virgin, your Mama used to do the nasty in the empty field where this here mall sits, with a man that wasn't your daddy."

"That's a lie!"

"I can prove it."

"How?"

"But you just said it was a lie."

"It is!"

"But I can prove it.

"Well, damnit, do it!"

"You're shakin', but hold on to your humility, 'cause I'm your brother."

"You are not!"

"How come I'm not?"

"You're a negro!"

"A negro? You died in 1966. A negro. Now that's a blast from the past. As if a *negro* can't be your brother?"

"You don't look like me."

"I don't smell like you either, but that don't mean shit. I also do not wear bell-bottomed blue jeans and T-shirts with 'GOD IS DEAD' written on 'em."

"Listen, young man, me and some of my friends blocked traffic in Yazoo City Mississippi, so you folks could have rights. So yes, in a sense we are Brothers. Is that what you mean?"

"I thank you for your sacrifice. Maybe one day a Church will rise up in your name, and we'll eat bread and drink piss in your honor!"

"Boy, if I weren't who I am."

"Your Mother don't mean shit to me."

"But she's *your* mother too, ha ha. You said so."

"Yes. Our Mother is a whore."

"Lies! Get away from me!"

"Face the truth. Our Mother is a whore. America fucks everything on this planet."

"Get away. You don't know me anymore."

"I slept with your wife. She tol' me all about you."

"My wife wouldn't have a nig . . . a colored . . . one of you."

"Ain't your wife got a mole under her left tittie?"

"Yes, but lots of women..."

"Ain't your wife got a silly name like, Gretchen?"

"Yes, but my wife wouldn't."

"Yes, she would. She tol' me all about you and your pitiful attempt to satisfy her—she said which is really an attempt to satisfy your own self esteem. Your wife, she ain't no airhead."

"My wife is a decent woman!"

"I'm a decent man, Daddy-o. I'm good looking and I don't smell like a toilet. Your wife tol' me, she said, 'I like a man, who likes to make love because it's fun. I'm tired of always trying something new.' Now ain't you heard them words before?"

"She, she, you've been standing outside our window!"

"Man, I ain't got to stand outside no window. I got the key to any broad's heart."

"I don't believe all of this."

"Listen Brother White, I eat green breath mints. Ain't you ever noticed my green circle around your wife's belly button?"

"You nigger!"

"Put the gun down, Brother."

"Nigger!"

"Hey man, is you callin' me or our mother? Put the gun down. I've done proved my point. Ain't no humble SOB in this world. God, ain't none of your earthlings humble. Not even your white civil rights workers who blocked trucks in Yazoo City in my behalf."

"Your prayers to God won't save you, boy."

"Ever'time a *boy* says God, it don't mean he's prayin'."

"Get the hell ready to die!"

"Well okay, but can I pull off my clothes? I don't want you to mess up my suit with them damn silver bullets."

"Shut up!"

"You remember our brother Jesus? They didn't mess up his clothes. At least let me take off my jacket."

"Hell no! You won't seduce me like you did my wife!"

"Typical white man. Thinks the whole world wants him.

"You wanted my wife!"

"True. And if you think about it, there's not a world of difference between you two."

"Shut up! You've gone too far already."

"Well, hey, Daddy, have it your way. I just got one question to ask, before you send me home to my father."

"Sounds reasonable. Ask."

"Did you really passionately love Othello Jones like you tol' me back in eleven grade English when you kissed me in the park?"

Punk'd out on Da Downlow

Now there's one thing I want you ladies and you dudes to know, and that is I'm not gay. But the other night, I did go to a gay bar with my cousin. That experience landed me running down the street, Buck Wile, buck naked again.

The reason why I went to a gay bar was because I was broke and my cousin said he would buy all of the drinks. I'm not one to pass up anything free, even if it might put me outside of my element.

"What kind of clothes should I wear to a gay bar?" I asked Lucian.

"Most of us will have on male attire. But you can wear a dress if you like."

I would have bust Lucian upside the head if he wasn't the size of Tyler Perry. Now when I go to a regular club where the honeys hang out, I wear sexy all the way. You know black silk shirt unbuttoned midway my chest, slacks that hug the hips, and very cute soft leather Italian loafers that I stole out of some woman's closet. They belonged to her husband. I like to wear silk boxers and cologne that enhances my pheromones. All of that's designed to attract the honeys.

"Oh, it will be 'honeys' at Club Envious. But to catch one of them, you might have to wear Celie's dress and cut that dick off and drill you a hole down there." Lucian cut his eyes at me.

"Nigga, you crazy. This meat wins first prize in every pussy it's been in."

"I know some studs with a strap on that will put your game to shame."

"Let 'em try."

"They don't try, they do."

That "Celie's dress" remark was Lucian reminding me of one of my other adventures. I always thought gay bars were little places with black doors and black windows with some dude in leather standing in the door. I don't know if I ever seen a gay bar because I never looked for one before. But Club Envious was right downtown a little further down from all the trendy spots dudes take ladies to impress them. In fact, it was right in the sights of *Chez Sous* restaurant where I took a chick once. I say only once because, fellas you can get pussy a lot cheaper than paying for it with a forty-dollar entrée and a twenty-dollar glass of wine. Shit *Burger Kong*, *Luby's Restaurant*, and *Church House Chicken* works just as well to trap you some good cootchie. But a lot of my boys still play that high-class restaurant game.

"Why are you wearing a hat and sunglasses," Lucian asked me when we got out of his car.

"Oh no reason."

"You trying to hide. You can run but you can't hide."

Lucian slapped two ten spots on the counter near the door. We walked in after he made me check my big ol' hat in the coat check. The club was bumping. It was wall-to-wall dudes—dudes in tight jeans, wife beaters and boots. Dudes rocked Armani suits, and some wore basketball shorts. And a few dudes strutted in dresses looking like they had just come from a dinner party. Eyes begin to follow my ass. I was not cool with that shit. I put my game face on.

"Damn cuz, you look like you taking a shit all frowned up like that. Let's go to the bar." Lucian led the way.

We squeezed by a crowd of niggas, and some squeezed by us. Now I don't mind a honey putting her hand on my waist as she brushes my ass while passing. But a dude? I was going to turn around and say something, but Lucian cut me off.

"You're in Rome, nigga. Do as they do before the Romans do you in."

Standing near the bar, a few of Lucian's friends saw him.

"Hey Luke, girl."

"Hey Fay!"

The dude ignored Lucian and grabbed my hand.

"It's Fabian and you are?"

"Uh, John."

"Nice to meet you, 'Uh John.'"

I pumped his hand one time and tried to let go. He held on longer than I wanted.

"Is this your new piece, Luke?"

"Nah, bitch this is my cousin."

"Kissing cousin?"

"It ain't that kind of party."

"Well, it's always a party in my house," Fabian winked at me. "Yes Lord, the blacker the berry, the sweeter the juice." Fabian looked at my crotch and winked.

I must have given Fabian a mean look. He stiffened.

"What?"

"It's his first time." Lucian said trying to ease the tension.

"No worries. I always use lots of grease for first timers. See ya later, girl."

Fabian winked at me and trotted off to another group standing and watching. I felt my ass hole clench tight as if it was locked.

"You gotta relax," Lucian said to me as we went and stood near the dance floor.

"I don't know why I agreed to come here with you," I huffed.

"Broke and free drinks. Plus, your Birthday is just around the corner. I wanted to treat my favorite Cousin."

"A damn cake would have been enough."

"Oh, it's plenty cakes in here tonight," Lucian said as he surveyed the room. Lucian was my favorite cousin in spite of him being gay. He's older than me by a couple of years. For some odd reason him being gay never bothered me. He even taught me a thing or two about women, what they liked and what it took to get one. I had been losing out in that department trying to be the nice guy and take them to dinner and bring them flowers. But not many gave me any play. I blamed it on me being too black.

"Yeah nigga, you black as coal in the dark. But that ain't stopping no woman. What's stopping her is you ain't selling her what she wants," Lucian said to me one day as we watched the Rockets game at his house.

"What's that man?"

"What's between your legs is what you got to sell. Stop wearing them Docker pants and them schoolboy polo shirts. Buy you some clothes that show off your goods, cuz."

Over by the dance floor dudes grinded against each other and twerked like hoes in heat. A few male strippers danced in cages and guys threw dollars between the bars like rain when the strippers pulled out their dicks. Lucian left me standing and went got us some more drinks. Dudes prowled by me like I was in the zoo. Eyes looked me up and down. Some smiled. I returned some smiles so as not to fuck up Lucian's game plan. I didn't want to be no dark cloud. Brothers and Sistas out there, If you want your club game plan fucked up, take a dark cloud with you who stands around frowning and dissing everybody they see. Bring a lightening rod. Just make sure they ain't as pretty as you are. I suspected that's the real reason Lucian invited me to come along tonight. His running buddy was laid up in the hospital and Lucian didn't really want to go out alone.

"I guess you doing a little better." Lucian gave me my drink. "You smiling like a beauty contestant instead of a constipated hyena."

"I'm trying man."

"Drink that Long Island Iced Tea and you won't have to try so hard."

That second drink was strong as gasoline. I know that shit was good because the vibe in Club Envious became smooth and mellow. I even joined in the conversation with Lucian and his Friends, especially the ones who looked like regular dudes. And it was quite a few of those. Very smooth very suave, could have got any girl's panties they wanted. One nigga named Jake seemed to hang with us the most. Now Jake kind of looked like my girl Brianna. He could have passed for her brother in fact. He had the same almond shaped eyes and a dimple in his cheek. And they both had the same honey colored smooth complexion. All Jake needed was some long hair. Every time Jake came around, my dick acted like it wanted to rise. I grabbed ol Eleven and held him down. I noticed Jake grabbed his dick too. Jake had that TI swag. I felt relaxed around Jake.

"Is he a punk?" I asked Lucian when Jake went to the bathroom.

"He's married."

"Married? To a woman?"

"What else is he going to be married to? This is Texas, fool."

Jake came back and we chilled some more. A group of real sissy dudes walked by in high heels.

"Look who's escorting Queen Lucian to the ball. Hey, Pretty Boy Red and Pretty Boy Black."

"Click your heels and ease on down the road, girls," Lucian said as he waved the sissies away.

"My heels gonna click over the backs of one of them pretty boys. That's what my heels going to do, bitch." They moved on laughing and high fiving each other. Jake said he needed a smoke and wanted to hit the patio. I looked at Lucian.

"You don't need my permission. You wore your big boy draws tonight."

Out on the patio more dudes and more dudes. Some were hugged up kissing. Any other time I would have been gagging. But I was cool. Maybe it was the alcohol and maybe it was the buzz in the air. Jake seemed cool. He mentioned he was married, and I told him I had a girlfriend. Said he was an Investment Banker with Morgan Sherman Investments, and his wife was a corporate attorney for Encon Oil.

Damn I thought. I never would have guessed that. Dudes with them kind of jobs at straight clubs be all Gucci and shit. Jake was real cool in his sagging jeans, white silk tee, and white Jordans. I admired his shoes.

"Shit man, my closet look like a Nike shoe store," he bragged.

Now ladies, don't get it twisted. Me and Jake wasn't doing none of that deep gazing in the eye bullshit. We was just a couple of dudes chatting about random shit. Jake told me Club Envious wasn't really his element. He just came out to chill. I told him this was my first time being here. Jake pulled out a couple of blunts from his silver cigarette case and offered me one. A few hits of that shit and I was fucked up. Dick acted like it was trying to bust out of my draws. Had to keep ol' Eleven in check. Noticed Jake doing the same.

"Yeah man, like I said, this gay shit ain't really me. I got me a cool ass porn collection at home, shit. We could be watching some good shit and getting our buzz on."

"Yeah man, that sounds cool. But I rode with my cousin."

"Shit, I got room on my bike."

Something about that bike shit made my head spin a little. I always said when I got me some money, I was going to buy a Kawasaki Ninja Black. They some of the baddest bikes out there.

"Really?" Lucian looked at me like I was a small child, when I told him me and Jake was going to hang out.

"I got my big boy draws on," I reminded Lucian.

"Well, I hope you can keep them on."

"It ain't about no gay shit," I hissed at Lucian.

"It never is," Lucian hissed back at me. "Jake, take care of my cousin. He ain't never rode a "bike" before, as far as I know." Jake nodded and threw deuces at Lucian.

Guess what was parked outside? A regal black Kawasaki Ninja trimmed in silver and gold chrome. Jake handed me the only helmet he had. I hopped on the back. Jake gunned the motor, and we took off as a few gay boys stood by gapped mouth in awe. Jake had to lean over as he rode. The wind whipped his shirt up from time to time reminding of Brianna's back. Sometimes Jake's ass slid back into my crotch. But we was just two boys on a bike. None of that gay shit. We took the scenic route. The buzz, the winding grassy bayou, the purring bike and the jewel stars twinkling in the sky made me think hard about Brianna. And here was a dude leaned over on this bike who looked just like her.

After about a ten-minute ride Jake pulled up to a circular drive surrounded by six four story glass and brick condos. Jake coasted to the farthest one in the back and parked the bike between two 528 Beamers. We got off. Inside Jake's condo was nothing but luxury. Huge white leather sofas seemed to melt into the white plush carpeting. Jake got a couple of beers from the double door Sub Zero refrigerator and nodded for me to follow him upstairs. We ended up on the roof of his condo. I could see the city skyline off in the distance. Jake offered another blunt and I took it. He picked up a remote and aimed it. Water rushed and filled up a hot tub. He started taking off his clothes. Peeled everything off and bounced over to the tub holding his blunt and beer above the water.

Now me, I haven't been in the close proximity of any naked dudes except for my brothers when we was little. I hit the gym sometimes and see niggas and white boys in their birthday suits. And being naked in front of the Doctor don't count in my opinion. But I told myself if I said anything or acted squeamish, Jake might think I was a punk. So I stripped my ass bare ass naked and hopped into the hot tub. Jake hit another button on the remote and a screen came down in front of the wall. Soon some hoe's jaws was full of some niggas dick on the sixty-inch screen.

"So how you and your girl get along?" Jake had slid next to me so we both could watch the movie.

"We aight," I said trying to be cool.

"Just aight?" Jake asked. His eyes were blurry from the joint and the late night. He reminded me of Brianna when she got tipsy.

"Yeah, we cool."

"Me and Maura cool too. That bitch love to give me head. That's my girl."

"Man, Brianna give head like somebody making her lick a toilet."

"Some girls do and some girls don't." Jake sighed. We both took another hit and downed our beers. We sat watching some brother eating a white girl's pussy like it had cream in it. Then I felt a hand on Ol' Eleven.

My first instinct was to jump. I thought it was some kind of fish in the damn hot tub. Jaws came to my mind. Shit. I know it shouldn't be no fucking shark in a hot tub, but you never know what trendy niggas be keeping as pets.

"Calm down, Dude. Calm down." Jake stared me right in the eyes. His hand squeezed my dick.

I relaxed. The herb had me under hypnosis as well as Jake's Brianna-looking eyes. Jake coaxed me up and I sat on the cushioned edge of the hot tub. He spread my legs and knelt between my thighs. I tried to push his head away, but his skull felt like a cloud, and I pushed against air. Jake blew smoke. I had to close my eyes to keep from falling off the edge of the world. I heard Jake spit and felt his teeth brush up against ol' Eleven. I was a gone dude as Jake worked my dick down to his throat back and forth. I began to moan Brianna's name as Jake worked my dick over.

Now Brothers sometimes things have happened, and we bury them deep in the guts of our soul. I thought about that nigga Kenny in High school who I let suck my dick one time. But you know, that was some crazy kid shit. I'm a grown ass man now and I'm liking this shit. Something in my head tells me to hit Jake. I swing but my arm is like rubber and my hand flops across the back of Jake's head pushing him further down my dick. I start to tremble and shake, but Jake pulls back. My dick is left throbbing and bobbing like it has a mind of its own. Jake's phone tingles and he looks at it.

"Maura wants us to join her," He stands and helps me up.

"Maura?" I ask.

"Yeah, Maura my od lady," Jake answers.

He leads me downstairs from the rooftop. We enter a bedroom. The room is all blue with blue neon sculptures of fish and mermaids on the wall. There are video screens all over even in the ceiling showing every kind of fucking you can imagine—threesomes, foursomes, all kinds of boy-girl and girl-girl combinations. Maura is as pretty as Jake. She has the same almond eyes. Her cheekbones are too high I think to myself, and her neck seems to be a little thick. But her smile dazzles. She reclines and her breasts are like large firm grapefruits. A white satin sheet is draped over her from the waist down.

"This is Buck Wile, baby." Jake introduces us.

She smiles and looks down at my throbbing dick. "I see Jake didn't finish his job." She reaches over and pulls me closer to the bed by my dick. She leans over, opens wide and takes half of ol' Eleven in. She rests for a few seconds before she's got three-quarters in. She works her jaws like a snake swallowing a rat. Jakes slips into the bed and sucks her left tit. Maura starts to squirm and at the same time pumping my dick with her expert head game. It isn't long before she has me trembling. She grabs my balls and before you know it I'm creaming her chest.

"A girl needs her turn." She crooned and motioned for me to get in bed on the other side of her. I looked at Jake. He nodded. We went to work on her tits—Jake on one side and me the other. The lights dimmed as me and Jake worked her over. It was nipple to lips and lips to lips. You might wonder how it felt to me to be touching Jakes lip with my own. I don't think I gave myself really time to think about that. The rush of sexual stimulation and Kush blazing numbed all of my senses until Jake's hand pushed the sheet further down past Maura's belly.

At first, I thought she had a dildo between her legs. My mind was trying to ask the question, "Why this bitch got a dildo between her legs?" Then my second question was, "Why was Jake sucking on a dildo?" But there was no third question. Jake stopped sucking and reached for my head. When my nose touched that thing, I knew that it wasn't no fucking dildo. Maura was a "chick with a dick." I jumped up as if I had been set on fire.

"What's the matter man?" Jake rose up.

"Man, it ain't going down like that."

"Ain't going down like what, bruh?"

"Jake, didn't you make sure this nigga was cool?" Maura asked in irritation.

"I thought he was cool, baby. I sucked his dick. You sucked it too."

"I thought she was a bitch." I said.

"Don't call me no fucking bitch." Maura leaned in bed on her knees with his or her big dick jutting out in front like a man's. What am I talking about? She, it was a man.

"I'm going to show your ass who the bitch is in this room." Maura fished under one of the dozens of pillows on the bed and brought out a snub-nose pistol. "You better pray your ass got plenty of natural juices, because I'm diving in with just enough spit to make my dick mad." Her voice had got deep like Barry White's singing *you'll never find a love like mine.*

By this time, I was heading toward the bedroom door. But it was locked with a dead bolt. Jake played with the key swinging on a chain around his neck.

"Come to Mama," Maura said as she followed me with the pistol aimed at my dick. I was backing up, knocking over vases and shit. "Ooh I see you like to be chased," "Maura" growled. "That makes my dick harder."

Now I had got myself out of plenty of jams before when pistols and knives had been aimed at me. But usually, I was sober. Well, I had sobered a little when I noticed the French doors. I thought to myself, "These motherfuckers lead to a balcony and that means my ass gotta jump." What were my choices? Stay in that room and get my ass wrecked and my manhood wrecked, or jump over that balcony with my manhood intact?

I bought myself a little time by pretending to play along with their game.

"Yea baby, I'm going to give you plenty of ass." I cooed and wiggled my ass. At the same time, I shot side-glances toward the French doors. I could see they were slightly ajar. I crouched low to give my body some sprinting leverage. Maura thought I was just bending over to get my ass ready for her piece. Suddenly I sprang for the doors. The balcony was short. I guess it was more for decoration. I paused for a second as I prepared to jump. I covered my goodies and aimed for the bushes below. I prayed they weren't thorny shrubs. Lucky they were leafy and just barely scratched my ass.

I heard a gunshot and knew I'd better get my ass moving. I spied Jake's Kawasaki with the key in the ignition. I ain't never rode a bike, but the adrenaline must have been kicking my ass. I hopped on that mother and roared out the driveway Buck Wile and buck naked on a motorcycle. It was dead in the early morning. Not a nigga, cat, or popo in sight. That machine throbbed and purred between my legs keepin ol' Eleven on brick. Damn! All I needed was to feel Brianna's titties pressed against my back. But nah, that would mean too much explaining to do if I went by her house. I rode until the sun peeped at my ass from the treetops. But I will say this, the next time Lucian asks me about going to a gay club, I'm going to bust him dead in his mouth and run.

Betty's House

Y'all wouldn't do white folks like that. I'm goin' to speak up for my damn money." Betty looked around for agreement and support from the tall, big-boned woman standing next to her. The Asian girl behind the counter tried to apologize, but Betty continued, "Y'all thank Black folks can't count, but here's one who can." The girl looked exasperated, took a dollar bill from the register, and gave it to Betty. Betty looked up at me and grinned as she stuffed the bill in her purse. She wore a grill over her teeth that made her mouth look like the fender of an old Buick. Her bosom heaved with pride. I turned my head.

Betty was a short brown toad-built woman. Her big round head sat squat on her shoulders. White stockings clung to her knotty legs. She was "ghetto fabulous" in her blond wig, green striped mini dress, and a shiny red purse hanging from her shoulders on a long gold chain. Betty's quarrel was with the "Chicken 'n BisKit" girl over her change from a fifty-dollar bill. I imagined Betty had a lot more fifties stuffed in that shiny red purse.

"Come on Li'l Bet, let's go eat our chicken by the window," said the tall woman. "Lil Bet" picked up her tray of five pieces of bird, a double order of fries, three biscuits the size of saucers, and a triple cherry soda and followed the woman. I got my Two Piece "Po Nigga" Special. The Chicken n Biskit didn't give a shit about political correctness. The Asians that ran the joint, sported grills over their teeth. Their grin was as menacing as a piranha's. The restaurant was crammed with hungry souls smacking their lips around crispy brown thighs and breasts. I found myself squeezed between Betty and the big picture window crisscrossed with iron bars.

I looked up at the sky and it looked like Old Man God had hung his gray drawers out to drip dry. It rains very hard in Houston in the evenings. The good weather the Houston Sunday paper promised us snowbirds from the north, turned out to be one soggy lie. The job's prospect was another lie. In Michigan, I made twenty dollars an hour slapping decals on the big asses of SUVs. So far, the only thing that boomed in "Boomtown" was thunder. If I didn't find work soon, I would be out of my hotel room and sleeping on the dirt. The manager told me this as he smashed a big cock roach crawling across his desk. I asked him was that worse than sleeping in a bed with fleas? "If you don't have my money by next Friday, the fleas are going to miss you" he said.

Old Man God let loose a couple of farts and the rain came down hitting the window like a sheet of needles. I ate my chicken by pulling strings of meat from the bone and chewing slowly. I figured the longer I took to eat, the longer I could stay out of the rain and the longer hunger would stay away. At night when I lay down, I could feel my stomach rubbing against my spine. I was that thin.

"Little Bet, John's sure been talking about you. He was at the club the other night calling you all kind of fat you-know-what's," the tall woman said to Betty.

"Yeah, he's mad 'cause I put his ass out of my house. Girl, first I noticed little dents in the side of my car. I asked him how they got there and all he could say was 'probably somebody at the club."

"I know you didn't fall for that," said the tall woman as she licked her fingers and watched me out of the corner of her eyes.

"I didn't pay it too much attention. I know how jealous our folks can be, especially when you got a Cadillac and ain't had to hit a lick for it."

I looked through the steamed-up window to get a glimpse of Betty's Caddy and was met by my tangled braids and long face. When I could see the car, It appeared like a hump of a whale painted red. Probably the last thing that rolled out of Clark Street.

"Hmm girl, what about that whore's perfume you was smelling in the car?" the tall woman asked in a sing song voice to goad Betty on. She had finished her chicken dinner and was eyeing Betty's purse. She caught me glancing at Betty's pursed and winked. I winked back.

"He claimed that was air freshener. Then last Sunday morning, I got in the car to go get a paper and I smelled something, kind of like dead fish. You know what I mean. I got out and looked under the seat and there was a pair of woman's drawers under there. Girl, I got so mad I..."

"Girl, people said he tried to make you believe they was his."

"He did, girl—talking about they was some bikini draws he bought for hisself for me. What kind of nigga wears lace draws unless he's a sissy? I threw 'em in his face. He started cussing, and I cussed him. Then he slapped me."

"Lord, have mercy!"

"That's exactly what he said when I got my gun. Girl, that dude went to hollering like he was singing in a choir. That basketball playing, he did in high school sure came in handy. He zigzagged one way and then the other. I was steady shootin. He'd jump ten feet in the air, then duck down to where he weren't no more than three feet tall. When he finally got out the door, I thought he was flying. I swear his feet wasn't touching the ground."

"Yeah, Jean told me she heard some shootin' over at your place, and the next thing she saw was John running out of there in his birthday suit." The two women laughed and touched each other's greasy hands. I made an ugly sucking sound with my mouth and looked out the window.

"Bonnie, go up there and get us another soda water and get you some more chicken." She flashed a big fifty at Bonnie. Bonnie obeyed. Betty's cellphone rang. She fished it out of her purse.

"Girl, ain't nothin' goin on but the rain. I'm at the Chicken N Biskit getting my feed on. Naw ain't nothing in here but hungry busters." Out of the corner of my eye I could see the flash from Betty's gold teeth as she grinned at me. I kept my eyes glued to the window. I caught Bonnie's reflection in the wet glass. She looked as if she was in a shower. Her back oozed through the straps of her silver halter top like brown taffy. Her rounded shoulders were just right for a man's hands to cup and caress. My fingers slipped between my thighs. The rain started up heavy and beat against the window like a mad drum solo.

The sun broke through the cracks in the Venetian blinds in ribbons of hot white light. Betty rolled over and touched my chest. Her damp palm made my flesh quiver.

"Who do you love?"

"I love little Bet."

I have been living with Betty, in Betty's house, for six months now.

Her purse dangling at the end of its long chain bumped me when she got up from the table that day in the Chiken N Biskits. Betty rubbed my arm slowly and softly. When she left, there was a crumpled wad of paper on the table—a ten-dollar bill with her name and phone number scrawled over Hamilton's smug face. I was insulted that such a troll would even think that the likes of me would give her one second of my time. I kept the ten spot and a little voice told me to put the number in my jacked up flip phone with the missing zero. I tell you; a brother is having a hard time when don't even have a zero on his phone. When Friday came and the eagle hadn't flown, the Manager tossed my things out into the rain, along with a nest of bugs to keep me company.

The first time I said that I loved Betty I thought a frog had jumped in my throat. My voice cracked and my insides fluttered. She wrapped her fat arms around my neck and stroked the back of my head.

"Who you gonna love forever?"

"Nobody but Little Bet."

I knew what was coming next. I jumped from the bed.

"Baby, I'm sure hungry. How about some bacon and eggs, "I asked as I slid into my pants.

"When did you start being so hungry? You know in my house; my eggs don't crack for nobody unless I say so."

I tickled her feet to placate her and went into the kitchen to start a late breakfast. It was ten in the morning. She finally shuffled into the kitchen wearing sky blue baby doll pajamas. Her hair looked like it had been in a fight with a cat and lost. She sat down in her red velvet dinette chair with its heart-shaped back. Her feet barely touched the floor. I looked at Betty and hated myself.

"You know baby," I said flipping an egg, "It's time I got me a job. I've been watching the Greensheet. It looks like things are picking up a little and . . ."

"You don't need no job. I'm your job."

I sat a plate of four eggs and five pieces of bacon in front of her. I tried to do a con number on her. I said, "My mother would die if she knew her son was living of f someone else's generosity. She always taught me to be self-reliant."

"You very reliable," Betty said nudging her toe between my thighs. I jumped backward.

"What you jumping for?" Betty looked at me. There was a slight hint of malice in her smile. "Ain't too many folks down here going to pay no Black man twenty dollars an hour to slap a name on a car. If I recall right, they don't make no cars in Houston. I'll give you a job though," she said touching my leg with her big toe. She laughed and skipped back to her bedroom.

I dried the dishes and swept the kitchen three times. I arranged the cans in her pantry in alphabetical order puzzling over whether green beans should come after or before corn. I heard Betty clearing her throat as if she was about to make a big announcement and knew it was her way of calling me. I had started on her spices—allspice, bayleaf, cinnamon when Betty cleared her throat loudly a third time. I was in the middle of her nutmeg. It was time to do my duty. I went back into the bedroom. Betty lay back on her round bed, shaking up a bottle of bright red nail polish. My breathing became tight and my jaw locked. She pointed at her toes. I took the bottle and applied the crimson paint to her cracked toenails. I had to use long steady strokes to avoid getting polish over the edges. I did not want to arouse Betty's fury as she watched two women pulling each other's hair over a dude with no legs on Jerry Springer. Betty kicked her heels up laughing, making my job more difficult. I squeezed her toe. She shrieked and rolled her eyes at me. I tried to smile, but my lips only quivered as if I were having a stroke. Betty looked at me suspiciously.

"You ain't got another woman is you? You're acting mighty funny. I'll kill you if I find out."

"I love Little Bet," I said like a mechanical doll.

"Well prove it!"

I closed my eyes and Bonnie's back as brown as a chocolate cake appeared in front of me. I bent over and brushed her velvet skin with my lips. I then turned her over. Her nipples large as blackberries drew my tongue out of my mouth and I tasted their sweetness. Her soft thighs held me tight around my waist and her feet massaged the sweet spot near my tailbone,

When Betty and I were finished, she rolled over and went to sleep. I got up and showered vigorously, washing her smell from my body. I took a walk toward the avenue where Betty said she used to "work."

"Know why I got so much money, Kenny Boy? She had asked me one day as she was cleaning shit off a fresh batch of chitlins' she had bought.

I shrugged my shoulders.

"Cause a man is a filthy beast," she said holding a hand full of guts under boiling hot water. "Ain't nothing he won't pay for if it'll get his rocks off." She was topless. Scars from beatings and bite marks crisscrossed her back like a road map.

"I paid my dues, and a nigga gotta pay his," she said as the funk from the chitlins filled the kitchen.

Betty's former comrades stood in front of an old crumbling building that had been a funeral parlor. They whistled at men passing in cars. One sat v-legged on the hood of a rusty hearse. She wore a shiny silver leotard. Her sales pitch was a slow wink at the passing cars. Her comrades were more vocal.

"Over here baby! Sweet Potato pie for sale! Hey sweet Daddy!" Their big thighs shook like jelly below their tight skirts.

Skinny boys on bicycles boasted and flirted with the ladies. They rattled their pocket change, grabbed their crotches and invited them to sample their boyish manliness behind the dilapidated building.

"Get away from here, boy. Your baldheaded mammy is calling you," the "girls" taunted them back.

Cops wearing mirrored shades, prowled in their squad cars slowly along the avenue scattering the women like chickens. I saw my reflection in their eyes as they gazed at me dressed in a purple warm-up suit that Betty had "Fly Guy Tailors" to make for me. One cop moved his lips as if he was going to spit.

I sat down on a box in front of the "Cafe de Paris." Hamhox all U cAn eat $1.00, was scrawled in chalk on a green board that covered a broken window. Dogs with more bones than skin nosed around for scraps. Old men on Lyons Avenue sat around spitting brown juices from their hollow cheeks and talking of a time when the place used to hop—when the girls used to shake and shimmy in their slips on stage at Duke's Place—when the undertaker used to have three or four bodies stacked in his hearse early Sunday morning following a bloody Saturday night.

"Yeah, young blood, the "bloody fifth" was bad back in the day."

"Shit you was a bad ass yourself if you made it back home safely. You had to have God on your payroll."

"Didn't your Mama use to walk you to the store?"

"Yes, she did because, because your mama was so ugly she scared everybody to death."

The old men hooted and hollered and played the dozens among themselves. I took it all in. It was good to see the sunshine again and be away from Betty. The smell of frying chickens, low mumblings and growls lulled me into a half sleep. Then suddenly there was a shouting in my ear

"Is you a man? I said, is you a man?"

I looked up, startled by a black bear of a man. Willy the can collector was hollering at me. He was known for his shouting and standing in front of the Powerhouse Church of God answering and signifying to the minister's voice spewing from the loudspeaker. This time I was Willy's congregation. He pushed his red shopping cart against a fence and sat down next to me. He reeked of wine and shit. He threw one yellow eye on me and repeated his question.

"Is you a man?!" The other white porcelain eye rolled around in its socket. It stopped and focused on a light post while Willy's good eye squinted at me.

"What do you think I am?"

"Don't git smart wif me boy." His laughter rattled, scratched in his throat, and made my spine twitch and tingle. "Now you see me, I'm a man. I works ever'day—Saturday, Sunday, even on Christmas."

"I work. I'm just laid off at the moment," I said.

"What they do up there in Washington don't affect me none. Look at my hands. C'mon, look at 'em!"

His bruised and calloused hands looked as if he had found them in a pile of rubble behind the funeral home. His palms were as black as a chalkboard. He closed his fingers and made a fist.

"Now that's a hammer, ain't it? Feel it. C'mon feel it!"

His fist felt like rough wood.

"Now look at yours—softer than a woman's."

"Hey man, I had a job. I was making twenty dollars an hour up north."

"What was you doing up there?"

"I... I helped build cars."

"Aww hell, that ain't no kind of work. All you do is stand there, and when your part comes down the line, you stick it on somewhere. You stand and wait for a piss break. You stand and wait for the boss to hand you your check. Uncle Sam be done stole half of it from you. Now me, I hustle. I live by my wits. I ain't worked for nobody in forty years. You young cats don't know how to hustle like a man. Oh, y'all put on them shiny suits and twist y'alls hair and try to hustle some woman. Some of y'all will steal or sell dope, just makin' the undertaker rich, that's all. Now look at you all done up like a purple lollipop. Is you what they call a Candy Man?"

"I'm much of a man as you are, Pops.

"Oh yeah? I'm gonna show you how a man's s'posed to act."

Willy grabbed my left arm and twisted it behind my back. I swung around to hit him in his big belly, but the fire in my joints doubled me over.

"Pick up that can there!" He hissed and applied more pressure to my arm. I doubled over.

"Put it in the cart. All right, now get that other one. That's right. Don't worry about that little mud on your purple tennis shoes."

Willy pushed me along the sidewalk playing street sweeper with me. A crowd gathered and followed. The boys on their bikes left the hookers and flocked around me and Willy like blackbirds.

"Aw Man, look at this. Willy got that nigga out picking up trash in his pimp suit. Hey man, you must be Willy's bitch!"

"Okay man! Okay, I got you!" I said gritting my teeth in pain.

"What, tired already?"

"My arm . . . It's going to break!"

"Oh, excuse me Mister," he said releasing my grateful arm. "I forgets my strength sometime." He squatted on a rusty bucket and cracked walnuts with his knuckles against the sidewalk. I stood massaging my elbow. He looked at me with his good yellow eye and laughed. I turned and stalked away.

"That's right, tuck tail and run! I's ruther be buck naked in Africa than some woman's purple play toy," Willy shouted. He got off his bucket and pelted my back with walnut shells. He made guttural noises as if he was imitating African bushmen. The crowd stayed gathered around him laughing while I slinked off in shame and anger. I thought about running home to Betty and bringing her back with her gun and shooting Willy. "But what kind of dude brings a woman to fight for him," a voice asked me. "You wouldn't be nothing but Betty's pussy." And she's already been hinting at buying a strap-on.

I found myself wandering down a quiet street that ran along the side of a graveyard. I stopped near some weeds to piss and massage my elbow and my ego. The site and feel of my manhood in my hands gave me some kind of reassurance. I shrugged off what had happened as being a victim of a crazy man. He would have done that to anybody sitting in that spot, I told myself.

As I started to piss, a voice called out "Mother Fucker." Then I heard an anguished wailing. I stopped pissing. I didn't bother to tuck myself in. I crept into the cemetery until I saw her. Her dress was hiked almost to her shoulders and a yellow stream ran from between her legs. She spied me but kept on pissing. I crept closer. My foot cracked a twig, and she shot me another glance. Then she looked down at my pants wide opened and my sex hanging out. Her eyes lit up for a moment as if she was scared. Then she narrowed them

"I come here every week to wash this nigga's mouth out with pee. Now you gonna be the icing on the cake. I'm a make this nigga roll over in his grave."

She pulled her dress all the way over her shoulders and laid across a dry spot on the grave.

"Come on lover boy."

I pulled my pants down and crawled on top of her. The sun warmed my ass. As I entered her. She began to buck wildly and undulate her hips. At first, I thought she was reacting to all the work I was doing. Then she began to shriek loudly and call out Alphonse! I knew she was speaking to whoever it was buried beneath us. She wanted to rock his grave and call down to him to let the brother know she was being fucked on his grave. When we were finished, I rolled off her and watched her jump to her feet and get dressed. I asked her who was Alphonse. She said her ex-husband. She said his woman put him in the grave and she wanted to make sure he had no peace.

"Isn't being dead enough," I asked her.

As she left the cemetery, she turned and gave me the finger.

The warm wind and pale blue sky and me all naked in it made my manhood rise up again. I got off of Alphonse's grave and dressed. As I knelt to tie my shoes, I saw something crumpled in the grass like a mashed up rose. I stood over it and saw it was the chick's panties. I folded them flat like a handkerchief and put them in my pocket. A few minutes later I was knocking at Bonnie's door. When she opened it, I started on her before she could get the door closed.

Well, I'm a dog sometimes. I have a brother who barks like a dog when he gets upset. I'm not like him, but yeah me and Bonnie kick it. Sometimes even in Betty's House if she's laying up drunk sleep. When we finished making love we got in Bonnie's old claw-footed bathtub and fell asleep. I had a bad dream. I was naked in some woods. At first some puppies trotted up to me and tried to lick me. They then turned into vicious dogs who snarled and bit at my privates. I awoke in a cold sweat to find Betty's phone number flashing across the cellphone she had bought me, and it was ringing like mad crazy.

I should have known something was up when Betty started frying her eggs and bacon for me. Sometimes She got up in the wee hours of the morning to drive to the Farmer's Market and get their freshest big brown eggs. She'd come home have the kitchen smelling like Denny's or IHOP. She started giving me pedicures painting my toenails in a clear coat varnish. All of this made Bonnie a little jealous. At least I assumed it was jealousy when Bonnie would say she's up to something as she eased me out of her house watching out the door as she was expecting a tiger to come pouncing in.

At first, I thought the hot water had turned scalding across my back. I turned to the faucet to turn it off and more hot stinging sensations struck my back. I managed to turn away from the water and there stood Betty with a bullwhip. She was swinging it like some cowboy on the Chisom trail. I heard it sing and felt its sting across the top of my head. I tried to run Past Betty, but she drove me back into the shower with a lick across my chest. Something told me to hold my hand over my privates. Betty came down with more licks across my shoulders. When I turned, I felt the lash tearing into my back and ass. I felt as if I was on fire. I tore at the shower curtain and tried to use that as a shield, but her whips tore it to shreds. She dropped her whip long enough to throw some red panties at my feet. She threw a clump of hair behind the panties and called Bonnie a whore and called me names too. Then she picked up her whip and said she was going to beat my dick off. I covered myself and cowered back in the shower as her lashes rained down. Suddenly I heard myself roar and scream. And like a linebacker I pushed past Betty with all the adrenaline in my body. Betty was right behind me. I ran toward the front door, but she had took the dead bolt key out of the lock. All of the windows were barred. I began to scream and holler like a banshee. Then I remembered the back door that was loose. I ran toward it scattering chairs and dishes as I ran. I aimed a shoulder low toward the door and with all of my might I rammed it hard. It splintered and let my ass out. Betty got one last lash on my ass with her whip. I didn't stop until I was a mile down Lyon's. Cars slowed down people on their porches looked and pointed.

CAR TROUBLE

I looked up and saw reflected in a distant mirror this hefty soft-faced man between two old, crippled women walking away from me. When they got to the corner of a glass wall, my man and his two ladies disappeared as if a huge switchblade had sliced them from my vision. I shifted my eyes to the left and there they were coming toward me, gaining height with each slow step they took.

I really checked this scene out. I mean what else was I to do? I had been sitting all morning in my yellow laminated chair in Sears' gray-walled waiting room getting ripped off by the minute. My mama's little car was in their big shop. All I could do before my Savior and his Mary and Martha appeared was sit and watch the clock on the wall. Except it wasn't a real clock as in nine o'clock, ten o'clock, and so on. It was a Sears dollar sign clock ticking off the dollars they were making off women and men like me with a mechanical IQ of ten. The clock started off slow because there weren't too many customers early in the morning. It crawled like an electronic snail:

One dollar...One dollar...One dollar...One dollar...

The next thing I knew an odd lot of souls had filled the waiting room and the clock was running so fast ticking off the greens that Sears was raking in; I couldn't keep up with it. Man, that clock turned into a jazz man's horn:

One one one one one...dollar!
One one one one one ...dollar!
One one one one one ...dollar!
One one one one one ...dollar!

That noise beat the hell out of my ear drums. My eyes got all crossed trying to keep up with the digital readout that ran like flowing red water. I was just too ready for a different kind of diversion.

That's when I noticed them.

My hefty man had on a pure purple lace shirt, brown flannel-like pants that flapped around his ankles, and brown-and-white wingtips ready to spread their wings and fly. He wore a vest and cowboy hat too. He walked right between those two crippled women. The three of them plodded like old mules. One lady was blue-black. She had on a white t-shirt with Mickey Mouse glaring from the front of it. Her jutting bosom made Mickey's ears elephantine. Her red stretch pants stretched from Houston to Odessa. She leaned on a four-footed walking cane and lumbered like a hippo. The other ancient puss was the color of my orange-brown man. And bless her poor lame self, when she sat down, her lime dress flew up, and her thighs went their separate ways. The chintzy wig sat on her head unruly and threatened to defy the laws of gravity. It shined like a swatch of oiled poodle under Sears' fluorescent lights. Old brown boy sat next to me. His rump hit the seat and stirred up a funny smelling breeze that sneaked into my nose and down my throat. I gagged.

"Man, I got me some trouble this morning. I got hands full of trouble," he said half smiling and squinting his gray eyes at me. His trouble started yapping at him.

"Bully! I say, Bully! You gone let your mama and your poor auntie die of thirst in this here steaming room? Get up off your behind boy and get us a coke." Her wig bounced up and down and all them gray hairs underneath peeped out and waved at everybody. Bully got up like an old man who carried his trouble in his rear end.

"I don't want no coke. Ain't they got orange Nehi? Bully's aunt asked.

"Lord Gladys, I ain't seen a Nehi soda water in years. Let Bully buy you a Coke or a Seven-up."

"I want a cup of coffee."

"Aunt Gladys, there ain't no coffee here," Bully half whined.

"There's coffee somewhere in Houston."

"Gladys, I swear, you sure is contrary," said Bully's Mother.

"Aw go on and get me a Coke. Shoot!"

Bully grasped both sides of the red and white vending machine and leaned forward. The shiny ass of his pants reflected a ghost image of the dollar sign clock. A keen-faced woman looked up from her crossword and frowned. "Mule," she said to herself. She tucked her head down and wrote. All the while Bully studied the selection buttons on the Coke machine like a man reading the names on a memorial. He dropped his coins into the slot, letting each one trip the machine's registers and make that electronic gargling sound before dropping the other. The cokes crashed down the chute like clattering bowling pins.

"Oh, Bully! Do you have to make so much noise? If you didn't want to buy the things why didn't you say so?"

"Mama, what do you want me to do, reach my hand up in there and pull them out? That's a machine. I ain't got no kind of control over it."

"Inez, I told you a long time ago you ought to have put a strap across his ass when he was growing up. Look how he talks to you now."

"Hush up, Gladys. Just because you beat your child into a cripple..."

"She deserved every lick. Bully, this thing ain't cold."

"Mine ain't either," Bully's mama said. "Neither is my heart."

"I doubt if you'll be invited to sit at any Saint's table anytime soon," Bully's aunt retorted.

Bully sat next to me again. His knee brushed mine because I was sitting wide legged and mannish. I moved my leg away a little, and again his knee sought mine. I got mad. I knew this lace cowboy was trying to invade my space. I had seen the likes of him lurking in dark bathrooms and gazing men in the showers at the gym. I had twisted my mouth to say something when I felt his soft hand squeezing my arm.

"Man, you want some of my trouble?" He half nodded toward the old women slurping their cokes but kept his eyes on me. I saw my dark self, reflected in his gray eyes. My mouth softened. There was an inviting nest of gray hair peeking through the open neck of his shirt. I swallowed and imagined my head buried in the down of his chest. A blast of cold air from the vent above us startled me. I looked at Bully's fingers on my arm like the fingers of an old brown work glove.

"Mister, keep your trouble to yourself."

"Bully, I want a chocolate bar," the old woman who was his mother pleaded.

"Bully, is they got a toilet in here? I told you I been taking some medicine. I wish y'all had left me at home."

Bully took his hand off my arm, but kept his knee which felt like a stone next to mine. The young cat's gray sparkle had left his eyes. He sighed. As the foul breath left him, his mouth was pulled down into a frown. His neck disappeared and his head sunk into his chest. He reminded me of my crippled cousin's doll that I had stuck in the oven and turned up the heat. She screamed as her doll's head melted into a goo and caught fire. Mama and Aunt Gladys rushed to the oven and fanned away with aprons and dishrags as the kitchen filled with smoke and screams.

I rolled my eyes at Bully, got up, brushed my ass pocket off, and left all of that trouble behind me. I was so glad to be free. The hot sun kissed my face when we met on the other side of the glass door. Then in all of that warmth, I felt a cold hand on my wrist. "Bully? Bully?" I heard a voice calling me. I turned and looked straight into mama's quivering face. I get up and unlock her wheelchair and aim her toward the bathroom. Aunt Gladys snoozes in her chair. The young man sitting next to me massages his arm. He gets up, snorts at me, and bounces out the glass door. I watch him race across the street daring the herd of cars to strike him down. When he gets to the other side, he grabs the front of his pants and struts down the street as they slip down around his backside. He's wearing bright red boxers. He cocks his head to the side and takes on a slow I-own-the-world hip swaying walk. I watch him until the heat vapors rise from the sidewalk and consume him. I feel foolish for watching him and thinking he could have moved me backwards in time from fifty to twenty when I had my Carl Anthony. Jesus. Jesus, make him go away now like you did then. You were the one who let the devil cut his body to ribbons in that filthy bookstore. The men oblivious to everything but their pleasure groped each other and danced in that boy's blood mixed with my tears.

Mama grunts and nudges her chair toward the restroom. I push and turn to get one last look at the boy—a red shadow in the sun.

IT BEGAN WITH DRAWERS

It began with drawers—rainbow-colored drawers that looked like giant flowers scattered across my floor. I took silk boxers and made them into beautiful drapes. Ratty "Fruit-of-the-Looms" that had tangled around ankles, I turned into baby quilts and donated them to Hospitals. I never had too many "Polo" drawers. I guess Polo wearing men didn't need me enough. They wanted other Polo men like themselves—affluent and well connected. I had to be sneaky to collect all those drawers.

"Hey, man, where my drawers at? Where my drawers at?" they would ask—shiny black ass glowing in the early morning light, cock jiggling and nestled between hairy thighs.

"Man, I don't know. You're the one who pulled them off. Look under the bed. Or were you wearing any?" I'd say coy-like as I massaged the balled-up underwear tucked neatly into my pillowcase. "Leave me an address or P.O. box and I'll send them to you if I find them."

One poor fella broke down and cried. "What will my wife think if I come home without any drawers?" I loaned him a pair of mine.

By Monday morning, I was sometimes washing a dozen pair of drawers from my weekend conquests. I hung them in the bathroom to dry. I sat on the toilet and recalled the bodies that had occupied the drawers—brown eyes that glittered like stars, chests that looked as if carved from solid brass or mahogany, and the perfectly round asses. Man, love isn't all the time about the heart and any of that romance writing bullshit. Sometimes it's all about ass and dick. I remember the juicy fruit breath that wore a pair of size twenty-eight "Joe Boxers." He was very college educated, telling me all his plans to get out of Roxbury, become an electrical engineer. He went on about the future house in Connecticut full of children and wife. Then he asked me almost childlike if he could still come and see me on Wednesday nights for his "special needs." I threw him out the house—without his drawers of course. I'm not a prostitute you know.

And there was that size thirty-four with the crotch stretched big enough to hold a softball and then some.

"Hey, man, where my draws?"

I shrugged. His zucchini size cock brushed across my chest as he flipped the blanket back and forth for a cursory search. He stood with his hands on his hips. He looked at me for a long time. His eyes slowly fogged over all sultry. His sex trembled, rose, and aimed straight at my throat.

"You got my draws somewhere. If you don't tell me where they at, I'm gonna beat your ass and make you suck me."

Jesus, what a crossroad I stood. Should I tell him or not? Size thirty-four made up my mind for me. He seized the back of my head. My mouth parted like hungry baby birds.

I have a room that is closed off—well it was closed off to the world—and in that room is where the drawers go when they are dry. I arranged them as best I could in a kind of artistic fashion on the wall—in fan-shaped or heart-shaped patterns. I hung some from the ceiling with strings like a mobile over a baby's bed. I sat in my gallery and read sexy novels under the leg holes of drawers. Sometimes I sewed. I took the older drawers that I grew tired of reminiscing over and made quilts that I donated to orphanages for the little babies. By Wednesday night though I'd get bored and be ready to go to the Ramrod to add to my collection. The Ramrod is a better place to mine for drawers. The men at St. Anthony's are too stuffy to shed their drawers. Won't get out of them unless you're pouring Dom Perignon into their Boston Loafers. Boys on the street are not a good source for me either. Their drawers are too funky and too full of holes and piss stains. I like clean drawers in my gallery. So, it was to the Ramrod. But for some reason, it got harder for me to mine at the Ramrod.

I lived alone. Didn't even have a cat or a bird. There wasn't a whole lot of room in my place. Two rooms, a kitchen, and, of course, a bathroom. A bathroom is vital to me. I like to be clean outside of me as well as inside of me. In addition to my boxes of smell-good flowery soaps, I have, well had—some good strong laxatives. That is one thing my mother taught me. Moses, you must keep your body clean inside and out. She gave me enemas every Friday night until she died. I was eleven when she passed. I continued the practice until a few years ago. In here, if I ask for an enema bag, a psychologist comes to visit, or he used to. Now they give me some little brown pills that caused my stomach to ache.

There certainly is value in living alone and having control of your life. I miss my porcelain toilet, my soaps, laxatives, and my gallery. I'm sure I would have had all of that until now, but I did something my mother warned me against doing. I opened my arms and heart to someone.

After my mother had died, I was shuffled from Aunt to Aunt, who felt obliged to take in Emma's "strange" son Moses who spent too much time reading and playing with his computer. My father left money for me to go to college. And since other boys thought I was weird (I called all boys, "sir"), I wasn't the kind they wanted for their gangs or their basketball teams. I was just "Ol' Mose".

"Boy, you acts old. Ain't your piss hot yet? When are you goin' to get you a girlfriend?" an aunt would ask me.

After college, I got my first and only computer programming job writing actuarial programs that calculated mortality rates (Southerners who smoke live longer than Northern Black males who don't). I always finished my projects on time. And I didn't go for that office party or after work drink foolishness. My mother always told me to keep my nose clean and to maintain a precise work schedule.

Well, Glenn—that was his name—upset my routine. I don't know; maybe my order needed to be upset. Years of thinking about things have changed my perspectives. I wish this shaking up had come sooner, like when I was twenty. The twenties is a time to be loose. It's easier to shake off bad lovers and go on to the next. If you wait until you're in your thirties to experience love, then the first thing that comes along, you latch onto. You're scared to let it go because you think, you'll never see love again as middle-age creeps in.

I met Glenn at the Ramrod. He was very black. His skin matched his black leather jacket. He was short and built ox-like. Glenn was a fruit-of-the-looms no-nonsense kind of man. He had large, muscled arms and his belt barely kept his stomach from oozing over his belly. When he looked at me, he pulled at something inside me with his eyes. It was more than a tingle between the legs kind of thing. I wanted to call him "Sir" lay my head on his thick shoulder and cry. His eyes pulled my breath out of me when we first met, and I couldn't breathe for a minute.

My Mother always said for me never to open my arms and close my eyes in this ugly world. To do so she said, would make me vulnerable to the snakes of this world. "Snakes pushed your father over the edge, and he jumped." Mother always cut the story of my father off at the point of his jumping. Why, where, how high up, and how far down, she never said. The vision I have of my father is a large black bird flailing away at the air. So when Glenn looked at me and cut off my breath, I floated in the air for a moment. I knew I would get more from him than his drawers.

Despite me turning my head (I turned it because I was afraid), he walked over to me and touched the center of my back, right above my tailbone.

"What's your name, guy?"

"Moses, Sir," I answered.

"I'm Glenn." He kissed me lightly on the neck and told me one day he was going to part my legs like the red sea.

"Yes, sir," I said. Tears were forming in my eyes. My heart was leaping in its cage.

For weeks, Glenn did part me like the red sea. He kept my legs as wide apart as the paws of the Sphinx. Things Glenn did to me required lots of cleanliness. I found Mother's old rubber enema bag. It was more rugged and held more water than the little plastic thing Glenn brought from Walgreens'. Plus, the soft vulcanized rubber felt like warm skin when it was filled with lukewarm sudsy water. In fact, before I started my gallery, I used to fill Mother's hot water bottle and sleep with it against my chest.

I locked the gallery when Glenn started coming around. He asked me one day why that door was always locked. I told him it was an empty room, that I had no use for it, and not even the landlord had a key to fit it. Glenn called me a liar and made me pull down my trousers and underwear. I'm happy to say that no amount of spanking ever made me produce a key or divulge the contents of my gallery. We turned Glenn's curiosity and my reticence about the gallery into a little game. Glenn became the daddy, and I was the naughty son keeping secrets from ("Daddy who gives you enemas, who cooks for you, who bathes you—and you lie to Daddy and keep secrets from him. Moses, I have to whip you. I whip you because I love you.")

And so, this went on for a couple of months. My arms were full of Glenn, and they needed Glenn. They loved Glenn. But Glenn—well he stopped questioning me about the locked room. His punishments became less severe. He stopped bathing me altogether. When I recounted my sins of the day or kissed him without permission, he shrugged his shoulders, or slapped me and slammed my front door behind him. The nights with Glenn lying next to me began to grow farther and farther apart. Soon new moons were coming and going, but no Glenn. I had no phone number or address. I searched through the belly of the Ramrod, but there was no Glenn to be found. So, I unlocked my Gallery again and made room on the walls for more drawers. But drawers weren't enough. Lord, why did I have to disobey my mother and open my arms? I bought more soap and more laxatives. I added mild detergents to the enemas, but nothing cleansed me. I couldn't wash the itching off my arms and hands. I needed to hold flesh. I needed skin and bone to caress and hold next to my heart.

At first, it started with ears. You can easily cuckold a man out of his drawers, but ears are another matter. To take parts off a body, that body has to be totally immobilized. Poisons took too long and were unreliable. They're messy when they do work. I don't like cleaning up vomit. The men couldn't always make it to the bathroom on time. Besides, I started needing feet, hands, even whole arms with hands attached. So, I bought a small twenty-two. Mother's old forty-five was too loud and left too big of a mess. As the subjects snoozed, drunk with whisky and sex, I shot small holes in their skulls. The twenty-two leaves nice small holes. I could wrap a plastic bag tight around the head and contain the blood. I wasn't trying to kill them; I was only trying to immobilize them. Hell, they could have gotten up and walked away after I was done, if they chose to.

Now I'm well versed in cutting up chickens. I used to cook for mother and me. I'd let the blood gel a little. Then I'd take a hack saw to the soft part of a joint. I chose short, thin men. It was a lot easier to maneuver the remains of a hundred-thirty or hundred forty-pound gentlemen into old Mrs. McKissock's trash barrels. Plus, it was easier on her back when she innocently wheeled her trash barrel from her porch to the curb.

"Moses, you haven't seen anyone putting stuff in my barrel, have you?"

"No, M'am."

"I swear this thing gets heavier each week. If I could stoop over, I'd see what's in it."

The gallery became full of an assortment of clothing. Nike tennis shoes, Italian penny loafers, Levi's, Tommy Hilfiger shirts, Polo shirts, and drawers galore. I thought about wearing the more expensive items, but somehow that didn't seem right. I dropped things into Salvation Army bins. The neighborhood began to sport some of the most fashionable winos and street people.

You can't keep ears, or feet, or hands as long as you can keep drawers. I never studied Mortuary Science, so I always had to have something fresh in the house.

Mr. Moses, what's that popping noises late at night I hear in your place?" I tell Mrs. McKissock the cockroach problem is getting worse.

"Ask the landlord for some Combat roach traps, Mr. Moses. We will both sleep better at night." I start wrapping the twenty-two in a towel.

There was a foot I hated to throw into Mrs. McKissock's trash barrel. Size twelve and toes all symmetrical, toenails clipped and clean. I remember his teeth, clean, white, and even like baby teeth. The first bullet woke him up. He jumped and grabbed his cock. I don't know, maybe the pain shot down there. I thought about sucking his cock one last time, kind of a final tribute, lightly you know, not as voraciously as I did a few hours earlier when I had made him tremble and buck from wall to wall. He was eighteen and gushed that it was the best blowjob he had ever had. He wrapped his arms around me and called me "Daddy." He said he could stay a while.

How long is a while? Is it a minute, a day? Is it a lifetime marked by stripes of misery and rings of joy? Is it Glenn who suddenly wasn't there anymore? I had thought about all of that before I put the second bullet into the boy's head.

Unknown to me, the boy was my undoing. He had made a long-distance call to his Mother in Alabama. When the boy didn't come home for Christmas, his mother panicked as I guess Mothers would do, and she got the police involved. They traced the call to my place. I knew something was wrong when a strange pair of blue eyes began following me around the Ramrod.

The eyes never smiled, never talked. Sometimes they hid behind shades, but I knew they were on me. At first, the eyes worried my stomach and made my hands twitch. I would lie awake all night. Or if I did sleep, I would be suffocated by the dark shadows that hovered over my bed. I thought it might be a good idea to stop going to the Ramrod for a while. But then I saw the eyes watching me in the supermarket when I picked up my fish sticks and heavy-duty trash bags. I saw the eyes lurking in the lobby of the Atlanta Life Building where I worked. I thought of running away, but something told me it was too late to run. You can smell your end coming before anybody else gets a whiff of your mortality. I was going to put a bullet into my head, but I just didn't get around to that. I had to rewrite a mortality table for Atlanta Life Insurance. People with AIDS are living longer. The insurance company is considering doing away with its Viatical.

To the world, I am an evil man. So, you want to think that my last day of freedom was one full of storm clouds, dark shadows, and thunder. It wasn't like that. I slept well the night before. There was a little banging around Mrs. McKissock's trash barrels, but I paid no attention to it. The next morning watching Mrs. McKissock getting into her daughter's car all hysterical, all I could do was shrug. I did notice how yellow the sun was for a February in Boston—golden yellow like old warm piss. Then there was a knock on my door thunderous and businesslike. I was in my vinegar smelling gallery sorting jeans to give to a homeless shelter. I knew who would be on the other side of the door. There were no body parts in the house, but still I felt guilty as if I was standing in front of my mother and her enema bag—very helpless and resigned to endure a gut-wrenching cleansing. I adjusted my clothes and checked myself in the mirror. When I opened the door, old "Silent Eyes" stood there in the sunlight holding a sheaf of papers. A squadron of blue men stood behind him. Some were armed with axes. I nodded my head and stepped aside. My body felt light, and I floated above myself as they ripped and gutted my house.

So, ladies, gentlemen, officials, Mothers, Fathers, and you the curious gathered to watch me die, it began with drawers. And yes, I am genuinely sorry that I've touched you in such a hurtful way. And, oh Glenn, Glenn if you could just hold my hand when I get to Heaven.

Kirby Bob Understands Heaven

"'Father, I stretch my hands to thee,' George Louse said before he gave up the ghost. Now he was a bad man—had chopped off people's heads and gutted them. He bashed in a few baby's skulls. But on that gallows' platform—him the rankest sinner knew how to call on Jesus. Now you tellin' me, Kirby Bob, little five year old Kirby Bob, who's just startin' out sinnin'—little tiny sinnin' of pullin' his sister's hair and throwin' her doll in the mud, and climbin' over the fence when I've told him not to—you tellin' me this little boy won't say the prayer his poor tired Mother taught him so he can get into heaven and walk with Jesus? Is you an imp that's growin' a tail, Kirby Bob?"

Kirby Bob had the thought to touch his backside to see if he was growing a long hairy cat's tail back there. But he saw something in Gretta's wide legged hand on hips stance that made him think she would believe he was being sassy. He shifted his bunny covered feet and said, "No'm."

"Well, why won't you say your prayers, son?"

"I'm scared to go to heaven, Mama."

"Scared to go to heaven? What you scared to go to heaven for, boy?"

"Cause you always say that bad man, George Lo...Lousy is going to be there."

"So, what that got to do with anything? "

The wheels in Gretta's head turned as she tried to understand the wheels that were turning in Kirby Bob's head. Her son had a strange way of processing the world, Gretta thought. This was a boy who arranged rocks and painted them and pretended they were planets. This was a boy who had stayed inside her womb all day and didn't come out until the moon was full on a Sunday night almost five years ago to the day. It was Kirby Bob who survived unscathed except for a purple patch on his left cheek, after eating a handful of oleander petals.

"What's George Louse goin' to heaven got to do with you?"

"Mama I just don't feel like getting my head chopped off."

"Do Jesus, boy, he ain't going to be choppin' no heads off in heaven. He prayed to the Lord to forgive him, and the Lord done forgave him his sin and made him an angel. Heaven is a good place to go."

"Heaven is too far away, Mama. It's just too far away."

"Well, Kirby Bob it is for some of us." She cocked her head slightly and thought of her husband Herbert in Miss Mandy's yard way across town raking up the leaves that fell off her chinaberry tree and singing. Gretta's sister had called and pulled her coat. The leaves, dead branches, and sharp dried berries from Gretta's chinaberry tree just blew all over their yard and stuck in Kirby Bob's feet. But did Herbert care about his son, Gretta asked herself? Hell no. Kirby Bob's life and soul was left up to her.

"You better get on your knees right now, young man and start to prayin' 'else somebody's birthday cake for tomorrow in my stove is goin' to be burnt to a crisp," Gretta said in a sweet way more to soothe herself.

After he had prayed and after he heard Gretta ease into her empty squeaky bed, Kirby Bob snuck out of the window. He stood outside and looked at the full moon. Next to him his favorite tree shimmied, and a leaf fell at his feet. A notion came over Kirby Bob to climb up in the tree and put the leaf back. He sneaked very quietly back into his window and walked down the hall past Gretta's and Herbert's room, and past his sister's room into the kitchen. He tucked a roll of scotch tape under his pajama coat and went back outside. He grabbed a low branch and swung himself up. He climbed and climbed and climbed until he reached almost the top of the tree. He taped the leaf to a branch that he thought had the fewest leaves. He stayed there a moment looking up at the sky and thinking of angels and heaven. He remembered the silky, glowing angels in Gretta's big white Bible. They had wings just like birds. He thought to himself, why climb down out of the tree? He had never seen an angel, or a bird climb anywhere.

The next morning as the sun and the moon sat side by side, Gretta was in her kitchen making coffee for herself. She looked out her window and fussed for a moment at the pile of rags lying at the base of the chinaberry tree. She knew Herbert wouldn't do a thing about it. As she strained her eyes a little more, something in her heart made her legs wobble. She whispered, "Come here, Herbert," just before her blue linoleum floor like a big piece of heaven rose to her face.

Red Underwear

I ran this ad, you see, because I was tired of being a lonely guy. For the last couple of years, since my wife ran away with her dance teacher, I've regretted the days because they catch me in their desolate clutches. I know I don't exist by myself on some vast island, but I am alone. Sure, there is the mailman who drops envelopes through the slot in my door; there is the upstairs neighbor's dog who whines every night at the wind, and there are the boys on my job at Zippy Delivery, who aren't too deep. I asked one of them, "What is life?" He said that life was pussy. That's all he could think of. So despite all of that stimulation along with the animal sounds of the city and the man and woman next door who beat on and love on each other until dawn, I was still lonely.

I went to the bars. But bar people try too hard to be cool and sultry, as if they're owners of the universe and their silk clothes and gold neck chains are vestments of royalty. I found myself silently berating them.

"Hi. My name is Henry," I'd say to some sleepy-eyed woman. I'd get a blank stare as if I was the smoke that they had just blown from their cigarette. "Probably just a hospital shit toter," I'd say to myself. But those negative thoughts only made me more bitter.

No, bars aren't good places to meet people if you are down to earth and sincere. Besides they sound like garbage can factories—"CRASH BAM BAM BOOM!" I don't have a loud voice, so I had to get really close to talk. I worried about my breath, so I always suffered from anxiety when I approached a chick. You see, I'm not too handsome either and the girls get righteously indignant if an ugly guy comes too close. I'm 5'4", skinny and bowlegged—I look like a wishbone when I'm naked. These glasses make me look owlish. If I were a Tom Selleck or OJ Simpson, women would have welcomed me to run my tongue over their eyelids. But for a guy like me, bars do more harm than good.

So, I ran an ad in a local magazine. It said:

LONELY GUY 5' 7", SLENDER BUILT, VERY NICE BROWN EYES, JUST WON

$1000 WRITING PRIZE—SEEKS SINCERE TRIM LADY TO HELP HIM PARTY AND

CELEBRATE HIS GOOD FORTUNE. MUST BE SLENDER. PHONE 881-LOVE.

Yes, I placed this ad. I meant to put a comma between nice and brown. I kind of worried about that. I didn't want to confuse anyone as to whether I was saying I was nice or had nice brown eyes. There is a difference. Lots of guys have nice brown eyes but will put their fist in a woman's mouth before she can say "I do." Me, I am nice with brown eyes. And that phone number, I thought it was clever. Now the money deal may have been a bit of a come-on, but I really hoped that when the dough ran out, I'd be left with a nice girl, kind of by default.

I'm a great believer in default. We are alive by default. We are the eggs that didn't die and wash out in our mother's blood. We are the ones who survived the pill or leaked out of a busted condom. And even if our parents planned us, we weren't the ones they wanted. We are what they got. So there's a lot of validity in the principle of default. That's why I was applying it in my quest for a nice girl.

Lots of girls called 881-LOVE. Even a few guys—the husky voice: "Hello, I'm Tiger. I give heavenly massages . . . "Of course, I hung up on them. But Like I said, a lot of girls called. A few were only interested in my American Express number. One lady said she was a Pentecostal Minister, had six children, was trying to start her own church, and the Lord put it in her heart to call my number. I told her that the person I wanted had already answered my ad. The lady broke out in heaves of sobs. She swore, when she caught her breath, to wring the devil's neck for putting rocks in her path of righteousness. The woman cried until I promised to send her a donation. She kept calling me and asking had I given God his share. I sent her a hundred dollars and never heard from her again.

Let me say this—It's strange the feelings you get when you run a personal ad. You're giddy with power and confidence. You dream of luscious women who are going to call, cry into the telephone, and say "I've been waiting to meet you all of my life!" All of that is what you imagine. You don't feel your own desperation until you see your ad surrounded by boxes of SWF's, SBF's, SBM's, and SWM's—all of those initials seeking love, and your own ad sticks out like a gout infested toe. You get mad because you had to resort to this. You had to beg for love and friendship. But you try to have hope. You make yourself believe you've done the normal thing, and you will meet the right person. Or so you think.

My phone rang late one Friday night about a week after I had stopped running the ad. I was alone working on a poem about a man on his belly trying to climb a mountain. It was a very sensual poem because I was using the mountain as a metaphor for woman:

On my stomach/I man, seek/Nectar from the throat of cliffs . . .

I'm really heavy into metaphor. Anyway, the voice at the other end of the line asked, "Is this 881-LOVE?"

"Yes, it is."

"I should hang up."

"Oh, no, don't hang up!"

"Why not? You already think I'm a tramp. In your head you've started undressing me, measuring my ass."

"No. I'm really not that kind of guy."

"That's good. That's wonderful," she said.

I asked how she found me since I was no longer running the ad. She said she was cleaning her cat's litter box and just happened to fold the page over and her eyes fell on 881-LOVE. I would rather have been discovered under better circumstances, but what the hell—I'm no Prince and this world isn't some magical kingdom.

She said her name was Ruth. I asked her how old she was. She said 182. I thought she was trying to be clever, so I got clever. I added eighteen plus two and I said, "Oh, you're twenty." She said no, nineteen right now in her present life, but she'd also lived previous lives as men. She went on to say she'd been one of Pharaohs boys sent to fetch Moses. She drowned but Moses got away. She died at 23 in a Chinese labor camp during the construction of the Great Wall. At eighteen, she was killed during the civil war—on the Confederate side. "And I've lived other lives. If you add them all up, they come to 182, Jack."

Don't ask why, but I didn't hang up on Ruth. Before I became a writer, I would have. There is something about writing that makes you accept eccentric people. So I played along. Ruth said she was mulatto, had a yellow cat named Calico, had a "professional job", and had had an abortion. Ruth asked me what color I was. I told her blue. She coughed and sighed. I was only trying to match wits with her, and it was partially true. I mean I felt blue most of the time. I finally told her I was Afro-American, drove a van for Zippy Delivery, and I was a writer. I added quietly that I was thirty-two.

Ruth said I didn't sound "Black." I told her to blame it on integration and white schools. My mother believed in white schools. Ruth laughed. I thought that was a good sign. If you can make a new woman laugh within ten minutes, you're on first base. But when Ruth's laughter turned hysterical, I asked what was going on. She said Calico was chasing his tail. I almost hung up the phone. But I thought about next Friday and all the following Friday nights catching me reading a book or wandering dark streets in my car. I decided to ask Ruth for a date. She said yes, after she asked Calico.

Ruth was definitely mulatto. She had pale skin, blond shoulder-length hair, and gray eyes. But her lips were heavy and thick, as if swollen with poison. I noticed a speck of glass in her right nostril.

It was a diamond. She sat on my couch, carefully crossing her legs. Her gold wool skirt rose high almost meeting the bottom of her black velvet jacket. The red diamond pattern in her black stockings traveled over her calves, thighs, and disappeared. She wore black velvet high heels with a large black bow across each toe, making her feet look like little blackbirds with wings. I imagined her hovering over me, gently lighting on my shoulders.

"Oh, you're so very dark," she said. "I'll bet you're very good in the sack."

"Well, I might ..."

"Be decisive. Either you are or you aren't. Which is it?"

"I am, I guess. I mean I am!"

"Good. But you're a terrible host. You haven't offered a hot lady anything to drink, you cuddly devil you."

Ruth chose red wine. She said it came closest to the taste of blood. After my fourth drink, my edginess began to dull. I asked Ruth what she did for a living. She asked me If I had ever heard of a "Dispatch Engineering Specialist?" I said no I hadn't Then she said she was a secretary in a large medical clinic. She had wanted to be a brain surgeon but was now reduced to writing letters to patients about the results of their brain scans or the miserable blotches that lurk inside of them and eat their guts. She said she hated doctors.

"But you wanted to be a doctor," I reminded her.

"That was a past life ambition, Jack."

"My name is Henry."

"Jack is more powerful. Just because you're a writer doesn't mean you can't be powerful."

"But ..."

"So, you won a prize for writing a story. How much of that thousand dollars do you have left?"

"Well, I ... "

"Oh, don't answer that crass question." Ruth touched my face softly. "You're so black and sweet. Are you writing a book?"

"As a matter of fact, I am. It's about a boy growing up during the sixties and seventies."

"I hope it's got pictures in it. I hate books that don't have pictures. One word right behind the other. It's enough to make you ill!"

I had myself another glass of wine.

I let Ruth choose the restaurant. It was called the "Pig n Cow." The walls were lined with the heads of pigs and cows. Tails hung from the ceiling. The waiters wore pig masks. A young black man in a mournful gray suit greeted Ruth with a wide toothy smile. He shook my hand and messed with some yellowish flowers on our table. Ruth said he was the owner and that he could make "looove" like a mountain jack. I sucked my teeth and scanned the menu: Oxtails, pigtails, chitterlings, tripe, collard greens, black-eyed peas, baked sweet potatoes, cornbread, bread pudding.

"A little provincial," I said and rolled my eyes toward the ceiling. Ruth said the restaurant was going to do well because the owner had leased the space next door to a funeral parlor. He expected a lot of overflow customers. But the restaurant was virtually empty the whole time, except for a couple of white kids in leather who eyeballed the walls and yelled "Gross!" to each other.

After I paid the very upscale bill, Ruth asked me what was next on the agenda. I suggested the Blue Water Club. It was "Down Home" blues night. "A good complement to the dinner," I said.

Ruth had a better idea. "Let's sit in on the wake next door." As a writer, I'm prone to sit in hospital emergency rooms to look for human drama. The screams of doctors, nurses, and the bleeding wounded—that's drama. I've never captured the essence of this in a story—not yet. I plan to, however. But a stranger's wake?

Ruth was insistent. She said death was spiritual. In fact, to her, it was really a higher life cycle. Dead people know the future. They know exactly when a baby is going to be born; when the world is going to end; and all the good stuff in between. The world is covered with these wise spirits and every man ought to honor them and try to communicate with them. And there is no better way than go to a wake and touch a dead person's face.

Well after that passionate speech, I decided to indulge Ruth I'd be derelict in my duty as a writer if I didn't try to understand this concept, this woman. And what the hell, this is a first date. But next time It's going to be the Blue Water, or I'll raise hell to the pearly gates of heaven.

Ruth and I walked into the funeral home and passed under the mauve archway. Along the wall a mural depicted the life of Christ—a golden baby laying in a manger; a man long bearded and tall, draped in purple robes, stepping out of a boat into calm blue water; and finally, a scarred carcass hanging on a cross—blue eyes livid with agony—wild like a wildebeest being devoured by lions. Those eyes made me want to stop and pen a few words about the frailty of man in the small notebook I carried. But Ruth's hand on my elbow guided me on. We stood at a high bureau and stared at the scrawl of names in the register. Ruth asked me what my last name was. I said Osborne. She signed Mr. and Mrs. Ruth Osborne in a very elaborate and looping script.

I said, "Hey, what about my first name? Shouldn't that be Mister and Mrs. Henry Osborne?"

Ruth gave me a sour look. "What the hell is wrong with me trying to keep part of my identity?"

My mouth dropped open to defend myself, but Ruth walked toward what resembled a small flower garden. I stood at the doorway and felt foolish. I didn't know any of those people—a huge black man in a shiny suit who sat off to himself, and a slender, light-skinned fellow in lavender sitting with six silver-haired women. The women raised their heads as Ruth passed them, then turned and looked into each others frowning faces. Ruth stood by the coffin for a few moments with her hands clasped in front of her. I saw her hand move toward the corpse. She turned and beckoned me. I shook my head. Ruth tightened her face, and everyone turned in my direction.

I didn't want to seem impolite, and I didn't want Ruth to open her mouth so I walked slowly toward the flower covered box. I nodded clumsily to the family. They stared at me. I looked at the thin old woman lying in her satin bed—her face sharp and angular as if it were chiseled out of burnt wood by some angry carver. Someone had combed a piece of hair across her forehead and glued it there. It was iron-gray and straight. Beneath this hairpiece, I could see her skull. Her eyes seemed as if they would pop open from some long nightmarish sleep. Ruth grasped my hand and put her head on my shoulder. I closed my eyes. I tried to envision a scene of a man and woman in love, standing on a cliff looking at the sun slowly dipping in the sea. I opened my eyes and stared at death.

Ruth led me to a chair at the back of the room. She cried softly. I patted her hand. We listened to a tape recorder crank out mournful organ music.

After they had taken their eyes off Ruth and me, the thin man and the six women cast vicious glances at the lone fat man. He did not look at them, but I knew he felt their eyes. He coughed nervously and cleared his throat. Every once in a while, he would utter softly, "Oh my God. Poor Mama."

"Stop putting on for your gambling pals back there," one of the women shouted at him. "You're not sad. You're thinking about how little her bank account is! You killed my sister with worry over your drinking and gambling. I'm going to see to it y'all don't get the rest of Ursaline's money," the woman turned and said to Ruth and me through her clenched teeth as if we had something to do with Miss Ursaline's death.

I started to speak up in our defense, but Ruth stopped me with a hard squeeze to my thigh. She began rubbing slowly brushed my crotch. I whispered in her ear. I said, "Ruth, can't we go to my apartment now?"

"When they shut off the organ baby," she said, "When they shut off the organ."

"Now I'm going to tell you something right now," Ruth said as she flung her bra on the floor. "I've seen every shape and size of penis. I've had two men at once, been tied up, fed canned peaches, had the syrup licked off of me, been spanked, have spanked. A guy even made me vomit on him. So, there's nothing you can do that will surprise me! You're all alike."

She crawled into bed. I crawled in next to her. But I felt I would have been safer mounting a Doberman.

"Ruth, you're not helping by saying all men are alike."

"But they are. Can't you do anything," she asked as she touched me. "Hurry up!"

"I feel guilty, like I'm violating you."

"Are you trying to pretend you're too sweet and gentle for this?"

"No, I'm not! I'm really a lion in bed. But you . . . '

"What do you want me to do?"

"To act like you want to."

"I didn't say I didn't want to. You suggested that we come here. I came."

"You put your hand on my thigh. And you touched me between the legs. So, I

assumed . . . "

"That doesn't mean I'm a whore. Why did you assume I was a whore? If you were playing football and a man touched you on your ass, would you assume he was a whore?"

"Ruth, what do you want me to do, for God's sakes? Do you want to leave?"

"Did I say I wanted to leave? Why are you always trying to second guess me? Can't we just lie here in peace?"

I laid there and prayed for the morning light to hurry away this darkness. I dozed to Ruth's soft crying.

I felt the bed bounce harshly. Ruth was bumping against it to wake me up.

"Let's do something exciting," she yelled.

"Swell, baby, but why are you putting on your clothes?"

"We're going to the 7-11."

"At two in the morning?"

"Yes, I'm hungry."

"I've got food in the refrigerator."

"You don't have Sno-Balls."

"What?"

"Sno-Balls, Baby. Sno-Balls—Those cute pink fuzzy cupcakes loaded with chocolate creme."

"Honey, I've got tuna salad, olives, boiled eggs, pickles, and rocky road ice cream."

"Well, a Sno-Ball is in my head right now. Get your clothes on."

I watched her poke out her lips and apply lipstick in one stroke, then she came over to the bed and kissed me.

"When we get back, I'll let you deflower me," she said.

I got up, splashed water on my face, and pulled on a pair of jeans and windbreaker.

The night was warm and humid. Under the nylon, my skin broke out in a musky dampness. Ruth clutched my arm on our way to the car and kissed my ear. I looked up into the sky. A beacon of light from a faraway Tower brushed the sky.

In the car, over a softly crying saxophone on the radio, Ruth spoke. "When we get to the store, I'm going to take off my coat, Jack."

I slowed the car to a crawl. I knew Ruth had not put on her bra or blouse.

"Why?" I hoped to hear her say she was only kidding.

"Because it's fun, Baby. I just want a man to be behind the counter"

"Now Ruth, if you're going to do something crazy, I'm just going to turn the car around . . ."

"I hate convention. Ten years of Catholic boarding school is enough! Sister, may I that—Sister, may I this—Sister, may I piss! I want to live!"

"Ruth, it's illegal!"

"To live?" she looked at me oddly.

"No, Baby, to be topless."

"You're dull. I thought you wanted to make love to me."

"I do Baby. My pants are about to burst."

"Well drive on, Honey, or else no nookie tonight."

"But . . ." Ruth kissed me again. I stepped on the accelerator.

"Sit here and keep the motor running," Ruth said.

"I want a pack of chewing gum." I thought if I went with her, she wouldn't do anything foolish.

"Just sit here. I'll get your goddamn gum." I slammed my door and sighed. Ruth looked at me and laughed. "C'mon, man. Get wild in your life for once."

I looked through the store window at the Vietnamese clerk. He had a small, pointed face and spiky hair. What would he do when Ruth took off her coat?

Ruth walked around the store. The kid's eyes followed her like a ferret's. What the hell could she be looking for, I wondered. Gum and those stupid Sno-Balls were next to the register. Ruth picked up a small flat can. "Cat food," I cursed. She walked back to the counter and smiled at the clerk. He gave her a sullen look. She turned and waved at me taking off her jacket. It fell to the floor in a dark heap. Then she turned back toward the counter. The clerk's eyes opened wide. His mouth parted slightly. I imagined him feeling what I was feeling in my belly and thighs. I sat up and hugged the steering wheel. I wanted Ruth right then.

She dug into her purse, and I saw something silver in her hand. It was a pistol. Damn, I thought. Ruth is carrying this joke too far.

Ruth nodded toward her purse. The clerk put money in it. She picked up her coat and made the clerk walk from behind the counter. She put her right hip against the glass door. I saw Ruth open her mouth and scream at the clerk. His hands went to his front and then his waist. He slid his trousers to his ankles. Ruth yelled again. The kid's hands clasped the back of his head. Ruth jumped in my car.

"Floor this SOB, dammit! Let's get the hell out!"

I put the car in the wrong gear and hit the curb. I heard the sound of broken glass.

"Reverse, goddamn! Reverse!" Ruth screamed. The car jumped back like a snake on recoil. In the rearview mirror I saw the kid reach for his pants. Ruth laughed.

"Wasn't that something? Can you imagine red bikini underwear? He looked too young to know about such things. I'll bet you don't even have red underwear."

"You just robbed a place! I thought you had a job!"

"Did you see how he looked at me? He wanted me so much, he was wild-eyed. Don't you want me?" She touched my face. "Oh, you're so hot."

"Ruth, we're in trouble."

"Not anymore." She opened the window and threw the money out. "Dammit. I didn't get my Sno-Balls."

"I'm serious."

"Don't you know how to have fun?"

"We could've gotten shot!"

"We didn't. Let's drive to the beach."

"Hell no!"

Ruth looked at me. "Why are you against me all the time? I'm just trying to liven up your white bread life. Red underwear. God! I should've gotten a lay from him."

"Ruth, you're crazy. I'm going to take you home."

"White bread eater. White walls. White toilet paper. White drawers. That's you, man. Black as the Ace of spades but drowning in the white man's morass of guilt. You're nothing but a guilty white morass!"

A police car approached us. Sweat glued the windbreaker to my chest. The car sped by, but I heard the brakes squeal. Red lights. I slowed down.

"Ruth, we're dead!"

"You're so dull. You're going to stop. You won't even let them chase us. No wonder you had to run an ad in a singles column."

I jumped from the car with my hands up. "She's got a gun, Officer! She's got a gun!" The police officers looked at me for a moment, then pulled their pistols and yelled for me to reach. Ruth got out of the car while both officers assumed a low crouch position. They looked like dwarfs easing towards us—gun-hands outstretched. They spun Ruth and me against my car. I felt iron cuffs clamp tightly on my wrists.

"Officer, I'm innocent." I felt the cop's knee against my spine.

In the back of the car, I sat with my hands behind me next to Ruth, also handcuffed, who had her opened coat draped over her shoulders. Two other cops came to the window, looked at her chest, and laughed.

I heard the cop that stopped us say he pulled me over for a busted headlight. He didn't know we were robbers. I looked at Ruth. She looked at me and smiled.

"You know, baby, when we get out of this, I'm going to buy you some red underwear."

I turned away from Ruth, trying not to cry, tears rolling down my face. The police car started to move. Over the radio a crackling voice announced that the robbery suspects had been apprehended. No more cars needed to respond to the Code One. The cop driving us looked through the rearview mirror at me and smiled. His radio picked up the voices of a couple involved in a fight. I heard a woman scream, "Bill, everything you touch turns to horse hockey!"

Love Feels So Good

"**I** am not a laxative," said my girl, Barbara. "You cannot use me like a purgative. I want your love to come to me because it's real and genuine. Not because I'm therapeutic and cathartic."

"Oh God," I thought, "Here it comes again. Like clockwork, like shit after Milk of Magnesia—Barbara's fit of consciousness because our sex isn't more than sex."

I turn and lick her ear shell. It tastes bitter. I lie on my back and watch the white ceiling fan blades spin quiet and ghostlike. Barbara starts up again.

"You think you are Gods—Gods commanding the world of women. Well, you're not Gods. None of you are Gods. When you're naked, you're puny. Puny, Axel! You Wall Street Gods in your pinstripe cloth—puny! Astronaut Gods wearing eighty pounds of silver stuff and flag patches—and I don't give a fuck if they walked on the moon—they're still puny! Soldier Gods are puny. Take away their bazookas and mustard gas guns, you're left with foxholes full of frailty. Don't forget the Pope, his bishops, and Cardinals. Strip away their brocaded robes and red hats; you're left with puniness at its highest. Gods? Hah!"

Barbara's jaw snapped shut like a trap. That didn't mean she was finished. She was resting like an anaconda's got to sleep in the middle of eating a horse or something.

"Are the Klan puny," I asked Barbara quietly. I blew cigarette smoke rings into ceiling fan's wind.

"You're not going to get my goat, Axel Jones. Hell yes, they're puny! I'll tell my daddy to his face, he's a puny son-of-a-bitch. And you too are puny. Trying to play the race card with me. It won't work Axel. After all, I am here with you. But I repeat, I'm no damned laxative."

"Stop comparing yourself to a laxative. You know you mean more than shit to me."

"Well thank you for your very kind words," Barbara said sarcastically.

"Just giving you some back."

"What do you mean by that," she asked. The sharp edge in her voice made her sound like a cat with a stepped-on tail.

"You're full of words," I answered.

"I'm a writer. What else would I be full of, besides empathy? Don't forget that."

"Maybe you're full of shit," I said. I recited a line from one of her poems.

"Wild ducks dance and die in the marsh.

The waters are heavy with dead ducks."

"Why you insensitive son-of-a-bitch!" Barbara snapped.

I leaned over picked up the telephone receiver and yelled into it. "Help! Help! Police, somebody has kidnapped my empathetic bitch! She was just here giving me a blow job. And now she's gone!"

A tornado hit my bed and lifted Barbara. She flew around the room gathering her clothes. She put on her bra so fast, she left a breast out. It looked red and embarrassed. Panties were pulled on backward. And words flew out of that girl. Out of her beautiful thin red lips, they swooped and darted at me like wasps. "Insensitive, lowlife, smelly, lazy, mind sickened by disease, and a sleepy little cock," Barbara spit them. They stung and bit, but I didn't flinch. Nonchalance and whistling are good antidotes for venomous words. Her voice turned to squawks. Her breath halted until it caught up with her tongue and for a moment, she gasped and swallowed her words. She stood in front of me, disheveled and dangerous. Barbara pointed a red fingernail right at my nose. She wheezed and gasped.

"Axel Jones, I've never said this to you before. I swore down in my heart and to my bones that I would never say this to you, but today you have pushed my nuclear button. Axel, you are a nigger!"

I closed my eyes for a moment and let the hot wind that hovered over cool. I opened my eyes and smiled.

"So, all of this time, all of this time your ass has been constipated with nigger. You were just waiting for a nigger moment so you could shit it out. Wipe my come off your mouth and get out of here."

"Axel, I don't mean nigger the way you think I mean it."

"Get out of my nigger house. That's what I mean." I got out of bed and sifted through the beer cans and Kentucky Fried Chicken boxes on the divan for a roach. I lit it, dragged on it, and blew smoke toward Barbara. A smoky halo floated over her head.

"I knew it was coming," I said gloomily. "I knew one day that word was going to drop from your lips like a loaded turd."

"Axel, I didn't mean it in a racial way. I meant the way you act, your psychological state of mind."

"Niggerology. Is this some new science?"

"Axel, if you were white, I would have said the same . . ."

"I'm a damned man. Look at this!" I pointed my dick toward Barbara. She looked away.

"Oh, you can't look no more? It's a nigger too now?"

"Axel! Axel!" Barbara screamed, "You're hurting me!"

"How can I be hurting you? I'm standing here naked, black and puny. You're a white woman clothed and majestic in your flowing blond hair. You're rich with your father's and Grandfather's heritage. How many niggers did the old man lynch? A baker's dozen? He baked bread, and roasted niggers, didn't he? I'll bet he ate a few too."

Barbara threw herself across my bed and wept. Her tears formed a wet spot the size of a small dinner plate. I left her heaving and lurching and went into the bathroom. My piss rushed violently into the commode. I felt a tightness in my belly and had to sit on the toilet. Afterward, I stood under the shower and sang a song I made up.

Nigger, nigger, nigger,
don't you cry.
You gonna be a
nigger nigger nigger
'til you die.

I sang the song over and over and louder each time. I filled the tiny bathroom with that song. It burst through the walls and pounded Barbara's ears. It must have gotten to her because I heard the radio suddenly blasting as if it were a thousand voices screaming. I let out a yell and a whoop and felt better. I stepped out of the shower, patted myself dry and tied the towel loosely around my waist. I sprayed Brut on my chest.

When I stepped back into the bedroom, Barbara was lying on the bed. She had stopped sobbing. She looked at me with curious kitten eyes. I turned the radio off, got down on the floor, and did a few pushups. I grunted loud and made sex motions as I raised my body off the floor. I stood in the mirror and flexed my muscles. My chest glistened with Brut and sweat. The towel dropped around my ankles.

"Axel, I love you," Barbara said as she raised herself off the bed.

"Shut up!" I snapped.

"Axel, please." Barbara came toward me.

I picked up the phone and dialed.

"Thelma baby, what's shaking? Yeah, it's your 'Axe' talking to you. You ain't got no wood for me to cut? I'll bet I can find a bush that's just dying for some thinning. Aw now, what you ask about her for? Ain't you ever heard of a social experiment? That's what she was. I know my place in this white world."

I stroked myself as I spoke. My pores tingled and sweat trickled down my thighs.

"Baby," I continued enticing Thelma, "I got a whole freezer full of Neapolitan ice cream. You can have the vanilla part. Just let me have all the chocolate I can eat. You know how hot I get pruning your bushes."

I looked up in the mirror and saw the shadow of a missile heading toward me. A pain in my head snapped my eyes wide open. I heard a crash. Everything turned bright yellow, black and then gray. A meadow full of black sheep grazed in the hazy daylight. A woman sat under a tree singing. Wind swept through the grass and the sheep scattered. I came to in Barbara's arms. She rocked back and forth and called my name.

"I love you, Axel. Axel, I love you so much. Don't hurt your Babs. Please, baby, don't hurt me."

Her tears dripped onto my head and streamed down my face. I reached up and stroked her arms. She hugged me tighter and sobbed.

"It's okay, Honey," I whispered in Barbara's ear. She lifted me and kissed me hard on the lips. I pulled away and murmured, "You know what I like. You know what turns me on."

Barbara reached over, picked up the phone, and dialed. An answering machine clicked, and a hoarse voice spoke.

"This is Grand Dragon Murray. We ain't here. If you ain't a nigger or a Jew, leave a message. Leave your name and address if you want literature outlining how to save America." The machine clicked, and Barbara's voice oozed over the line.

"Daddy, Axel is screwing me, and it feels so good. Ooh daddy, don't you wish you had some? It feels so good." Barbara let the phone drop. "It feels so good, Axel. Love feels so good," she crooned softly.

"Here it comes again," I sighed. I licked Barbara's ear shell.

How I Got Over

...Getting up at 6 to watch you sing at 7—
     You and your white-robed cohorts shimmer
and sway across the gray video screen—
How I got o-over
My soul looks back and wonders
How I got over
The night before, you fooled me to an arena.
Next to watery glass doors, I stood like Lot's wife.
With Rocket's tickets in my hand,
I watched schools of people swim by me.
Through my glazed eyes, I counted heads.
But not one belonged to you. Not one was your smug mask.
The next day you smiled through bone-white teeth and said,

  "Baby, don't you remember?
  I said I couldn't make it.
  Are you crazy or what?
  I would never have stood there all night."

But i loved you, man and pretended i was forgetful.
Getting up at 6 to watch you sing at 7-
You and your choir weave left and right
Like a forest of red trees under the spell of the east wind.
Two weeks ago i gave you money
So you could ride to that place,
St. Pious Holy Baptist Church—" Built to the Glory of God!"—

In your new crimson robes, in your ice blue Thunderbird.
There you prayed the sinner's prayer:

  "Lord Jesus, I am unworthy to walk this earth,
  And I know it. But rain down salvation anyway
  On my burning flesh—on my rotting corpse.

No man knew your disease,
But it was I, woman, who saved you from your minor hell.
The repo man was at your thin heels
Ready to hook his hook to the underbelly
Of your shiny metal ego.
You held him off with my lucre.
The next day, you called me an idiot and hung up in my ringing
ears.
I had asked you for a dollar
So i could ride the bus to my gig
Deep in the soft belly of EXXON Company, USA.
I use a computer. You use me.
                "How I got o-over.
          My soul looks back and wonders,
                How I got o-over."

My Mother is ill. Cancer is slowly eating her eggs.
      But she said I was sicker than her for fooling with you.
I said, "But Mama, I love his brown eyes."
She said those wet slanted eyes belong to a fox,
A hen eater, a tail-between-the-legs dog.
I looked down at my feet and saw them chewed and bleeding.
When you called my Mama a bloated cow to my face,
I told myself it was because your mother had tried to abort you.

But the coat hanger caught your twin sister instead,
And you had to live in the dark shadows of that woman's
disappointment.
That is why you hate me, my Mama, all women.

> *"How I got o-over,*
> *My soul looks back and wonders,*
> *How I got o-over."*

Standing before you naked, you laughed at my breasts.
Said they were nothing more than peanuts,
And I was cheap, my ass was too big,
My thighs too long,
I had hair like a dog's, and smelled like one—How
Could i expect <u>you</u> to get it up for somebody as ugly as me?
You spat those words in my face so softly.
And I stood shivering in front of your limp cock-
Shivering in your room walled with blond Playboy centerfolds,
Shivering under your burning gaze—my mind asking me
if I dyed my hair, would that make a difference?

Getting up at 6 to watch you sing at 7,

> *"How I got o-over,*
> *My soul looks back and wonders,*
> *How I got o-over."*

Baby, i bought you that cherry-red suit
And alligator slippers to match, last Christmas.
You gave me a $1.98 box of candy

And a card with a black Santa Claus exposing himself.

It said, "Merry Xmas. Have a peppermint, Baby."

I just laughed and said, "Oh how clever."

While you ate my Mama's turkey breast under her watchful eye.
Her eye that asked me, "Fool, when you gonna wake up?"
i tipped into your unlocked 3rd floor honeycomb,
And smelled love, heard it growling in your bedroom.
There you were in bed with a young boy—Tongue to tongue, pelvis to pelvis.
In the hazed mirror i saw your ass twitching
Like the jaws of a nervous old man.
You said, stroking this baby's soft curls,
That he was so much finer than I
And then you kissed him on his forehead.
For people weak as water, as I am,
We leave revenge up to God.
They told me as you lay dying from AIDS, scalding sores
Erupted on your ass and chest, like little volcanoes.
You jerked like a monkey full of pepper
And cried for me and God to rub ointment on your wounds,
But I was in God's house, singing.
When I get through singing on Sunday mornings,
I leave Stone Church
And wait for the robe of darkness to cover the sky.
In the graveyard, with evergreens as my witnesses,
I lift my dress and wash your mouth-
Your ugly mouth locked in a death grin—
I wash it until my bladder collapses dry and dusty as my heart.

> *"How I got o-over.*
> *My soul looks back and wonders,*
> *How I got o-over."*

Unfucked

Maura reached to unlock her front door
    Of wood and stained glass,
Of dreams, empty hearts, and
Lips unrequited.
A sliver of light between door and jamb stopped her.
She turned and looked at Sidney's car parked in the drive.
"I've told that man a million times to lock this door.
He left enough room for demons and snakes to enter."
Maura shut the door with a soft click.
Sidney's briefcase sat where he normally parked it,
On the bottom step of the winding stairs.
Her husband,
That—"*Everything has a place*"—man
a knot of contradictions—
Neat with furniture, careless with lives, even his own.
"But that's a man," Maura sighed.
She threw her purse on the couch and started to yell Sidney's name,
But changed her mind. He was no doubt playing
Some silly game on the computer and wouldn't answer.
"That's a man too—responding only to dinner and pussy."
Maura was thirsty.
Her drive home drained her of all liquid except blood
And the heat had parched her lips.
She slipped into her silent kitchen.
Two glasses sat on the counter—
One half full one half empty.
That was Sidney's favorite riddle.

And he was a man of riddles.
He could love her all day with words
And birdlike pecks on the cheek
But leave her unfucked at night.
As fresh water splashed into her clean glass,
She thought she heard a moan.
"The devil," Maura said to herself, cocked her head, and listened.
Silence.
"What's there to say in the house of an unfucked woman?
What are these walls whispering about?
Nothing at all." She sighed and continued filling her glass.
As she drank, a voice cried out, "Fuck me into jelly!"
"Surely that's the devil, but what does he want with me?
Jezebel doesn't live in this tomb of chrome and glass,
Of pecks on the cheek and a twat untouched.
What does the devil want with me?"
Maura stood at the stairs leading to her bedroom.
And pondered over Lucifer, who by now
Had groaned four times like a man in the gas chamber.
She looked at her watch. It was only four in the afternoon.
Perhaps she should have warned Sidney she was getting off early.
Could he be in bed with a bottle of champagne,
And her panties on his head like a crown?
She had seen that act in a magazine.
But that woman got fucked. Even the champagne bottle
Had gotten into the act.
"How is it that a bottle can be more fun than a man?"
She had wondered then. Now she knew.
Maybe Sidney was taking care of some of his
Man business. Maura had peeped him once in the bathroom,
In the wee hours of the night while she was supposed to be asleep —
Saw him spilling his seed into the toilet.

With eyes squeezed together, he reminded her of a man
Betting his life on a roll of dice in a game of craps.
"All of those children going to drown in the clean toilet,"
She said as she touched her belly.
Maura tipped up the stairs,
Got halfway and "*Bitch*!" stopped her.
She looked over her shoulder,
"Surely the devil is in these walls mocking me."
A hand slapped against flesh. More sighs and moans
Tumbled down the stairs to where she stood
By the painting of *Butterflies Fluttering Among Pomegranates*
Oozing seed and blood.
The voice was unfamiliar—deeper than Sidney's.
The tongue might have been attached to a ghetto street corner,
Or James Earl Jones.
Maura wondered if she was dreaming, and should she hike her
dress—
Hike it to the sky and let the garment float away like a kite.
By now she was at the top of the stairs.
Standing by the *Montage of Bees Buzzing Through Sunflowers*.
This was Sidney's favorite painting. Splashes of yellow and black
burst
Through the white walls and made her dizzy.
Their bedroom door was ajar—so like that peck on the cheek
Sidney.
"Maybe he was in the spare room watching porn," Maura thought.
Porn was something men did, she supposed.
Porn—jack-off in the toilet, rinse, and repeat,
Leave the wife unfucked.
She started to let Sidney have his moment.
But thought about the two glasses on the counter—
One half full, one half empty.

Maura stood at the doorway to their bedroom.
Moans and sighs sang in her ears. Her breathing slowed.
She wondered why that bitch's twat was getting fucked
While hers lay discarded like a dead fish in the mud.
The tall *African Fertility Sculpture*, with jutting breasts and moon face,
Beckoned from her stone pedestal.
"Make me your sword, so that I may smite that whore."
Maura paid no attention.
After all, despite his contradictions,
Sidney filled up the space around her,
Opened tight jars and carried the heavier bags of groceries.
He liked her spaghetti and called her "honey."
They did a little sex thing every other Friday.
He was enough husband.
Fertility laughed and shook her head.
"Enough husband," she mocked Maura.
Maura tossed all reasoning aside,
Snatched *Fertility* off her pedestal,
And pushed open the door
Enough to stick her head and shoulders in,
Like a cat peering around a corner.
The first thing Maura saw was Sidney's feet high in the air,
As if he was flying on a playground swing.
She noticed how clean and pink his soles looked—like child's feet.
She toured past the foot, ankle,
Down his tan leg, and past his knee shaped like a red potato.
Her eyes suddenly shifted to the mirror hanging above the dresser.
She couldn't look directly at the ass gyrating between her husband's knees.
It seemed rude to stare at the winking eye
In the middle of the Devil's black ass.

Below the buttocks hung the Devil's horse cock,
Sweating, drilling deep into Sidney.
All night long. All night long.
While Maura stood unfucked
Holding onto *Fertility*.

No Satisfaction

At eleven o'clock
    Edgar naked and black
bathes himself with moonlight,
gently brushes his shoulders
with rose petals,
fans with palm leaves
He is not satisfied.
His soul is hot
He rubs thorns across his nipples
until they bleed red tears,
sprinkles crushed pepper
into his open asshole.
In his orgasmic fever
he whispers the names of God
from Allah to Yahweh
then remembers it is not Sunday.
He puts on his evening gown.
It is gold and glittering.
He girds his loins with
the skins of rainbow Diamondbacks,
wraps slithering cobras
around his hooves
and covers his eyes with dark facades.
He steps out.
Watch out, boys,
Edgar steps out.
Whirling blue balls greet him

When he strides into
the *Black Platinum*.
Men and pseudo men
drawn to the gold
quiz him. His paradox
is an aphrodisiac.
His malice is disguised as sex appeal.
Eyes pry open
his long legs—legs where
soldiers and horses have traveled
for decades. Who could know this?
The pancake batter on his face
distorts his history.
He throws out his hook hands

   that sigh with rubies and emeralds.

He lures one chicken.
He is young and doesn't know
how many miles he must walk
from his shaved head
to his lizard skinned boots.
He just knows his dick is hard
and that's making him hard up.
If he doesn't get any satisfaction
he may have to take his gat
shopping at Seven Eleven and trade a few bullets
for blood and Winston's
And how long does that rush last
he asks himself?
Edgar takes him home.
His room is dark
but he pulls down shades.

Their clothes drop to the floor
like splattering blood.
The young root enters too quickly.
Edgar had hoped for prolonged stories
written by traveling fingers.
He bites the ear of the chicken
to slow him down,
rolls him on his back.
His tongue bathes him and lips
suckle him in orifices
his Mama has forgotten.
The young buck moans out love songs
that mimic whispering saxophones.
This from a boy whose longest
conversation was "Yo, wha's up, Gee?"
But Edgar has him singing hallelujah praises.
Edgar is not satisfied
He envies the boy's pleasure—
His selfish young man pleasure.
He sees him rolling off
To sleep after dropping seeds
On his thighs and sheets.
For meanness and to make it all
About him, Edgar bites off the boy's dick.
When all blood and electrical spasms
Drains from the young body
Edgar stuffs him one piece at a time
Up his ass
Until his belly swells.
The next day he calls his Mama
and reports how pregnant he is.
He says he is happy

he is going to be a Mother
and how he can't wait to
birth his baby and dip
him in scalding water.

(From Christmas in Linken Park Chicago)

The Fate of the Nutcracking Midget and Mud Turtle Mississippi

"Well first of all it's Christmas day and no Butcher wants you coming around banging on his door. Ain't that right, Dog2020?"

"You sho, right, Madd. Pass some of that grease and cornbread dressing."

"Then the next thing is where in hell is the butcher going to find a huge ass turkey?"

"Unless he went to Turkey?"

"What you talking about, Dog2020?"

"Well, ain't Turkey where they got a lot of turkeys?"

"Fool, Turkey ain't got no turkeys. It's the people that call themselves Turkey. It's a country."

"Madd, now you sounding like a fool. Why would anybody call themself a turkey, or live in a place called Turkey, without any turkeys? I know a lot of country people and ain't none of them that dumb. I think you done had too much of Ebenezer's free liquor."

"Dog2020, shut your ass up and let me finish. Can you do that? Anyway, the Butcher tried to explain that he was closed and besides the only meat he had was an oxtail the size of a possum's nose and about the same color. Well, the midget showed the Butcher the box of money. Suddenly, all kinds of possibilities were opened up."

"You sho right, Madd. I met Halle Berry one night over at the Drop Out Bar."

"You telling a lie before your tongue can get to moving."

"I swear on a stack of Bibles and Jehovah Witness literature. I met Halle Berry at the Drop Out Bar, right there on Obama Avenue."

"And just what happened?"

"I offered to buy her a drink. She turned me down at first. Then I showed her my shoebox of money and it opened all of them possibilities. In fact, we made it over to the Dew Drop Inn and she showed me just what possibility was possible. Yep, I know all about possibilities opening up."

"It's Christmas. I know if the Lord wasn't busy celebrating, he'd reach down and slap you upside the head for that lie. Anyway, that Butcher sized up money and he sized up the midget. He sized up the money and he sized up the midget. He sized..."

"How many times you going to say that, Madd. Your mouth sounds like a broken record."

"I'm trying to lend atmosphere to the story."

"I hope there ain't no farting in the story. We don't need that kind of atmosphere. "

"I heard after they buried your Mama, they still hear her farting from the grave."

"Don't talk about my dead Mama. Don't talk about my Mama, like that."

"Put that pocketknife down, before I pick your teeth with it. Besides your Mama ain't even dead yet."

"Oh, that's right. Sorry about that, Madd."

"But if she was dead, she wouldn't stop farting."

"Watch out now!"

"That Butcher sized up everything and determined that the midget was about the size of a nice size turkey. He wouldn't need to pluck any feathers off the thing. Plus he could pass that big head off as a hog's head."

"That hoghead cheese give me gas."

"Everything give you gas. Crackers give you gas."

"You sure right. Remember that time in 1956 when them Mississippi crackers almost gave us the shits?"

"Now why you want to bring that up in the middle of this nice Christmas story? We almost at the end too."

"Well, you the one mentioned gas and crackers"

"I'd like to forget that."

"I would too but my back still hurts."

"And my ribs are still dislocated. That's why I been gettin' a government check for forty years."

"Why my Mama send me down to visit her folks in Mud Turtle Mississippi, I'll never know."

"And why my Mama thought it was a good idea if I tagged alone, made even less sense. Especially after what happened to Emmett Till. She talkin' about fresh country air would be good for me. Fresh country air like to have killed my ass."

"Mud Turtle Mississippi. Lord, it was against the law for a black man to even blink his eyes if a white woman was around."

"First thing we noticed when we got from the top of the Greyhound bus was every black man walking around with eyes bugged out like Orphan Annie's."

"We should've walked back home when that Bus Driver told us Black folk weren't even permitted to ride inside a Greyhound bus approaching Mud Turtle."

"Lord yes—couldn't even ride inside the bus. We men had a time getting that poor old sister up that ladder."

"It didn't help that she had a bad bladder and had ate a bowl of pinto beans for lunch."

"Didn't help my nose at all. But we got her up there and we rode into Mud Turtle looking like crows on a telephone line."

"And then we couldn't get off the bus until all the white folks got off and had drove out of town."

"The clock was striking midnight when the Sheriff allowed us off that bus."

"And Mud Turtle was about as muddy as its name."

"Sure was. We found out a lot more when your Aunty sent us to the Post Office to buy one stamp."

"We use to wonder why we'd get her Christmas Cards in March. Black folk weren't allowed to buy but one stamp a day and mail one letter a day. And you couldn't mail a letter on the same day you bought the stamp."

"Them white folks in Mud Turtle kept their feets pressed to the black man's neck."

"Kept their feet anywhere on the black man. You know at first, I thought that Sheriff was asking a rhetorical question."

"What kind of question is that, Madd?"

"It's a question that ain't about the answer."

"Why would anybody ask a question if they didn't want an answer?"

"Sometimes people want to think."

"Why ask a question if you want to think? I'd just keep the question unasked so I could keep thinking about it. I ask a question because I want to stop thinking about it."

"Listen I been to college, so I know all about rhetoric."

"You learn all of that in them two weeks you spent at the Morehouse Cooking School?"

"That sounds like a rhetorical question that don't need no answer. So, when that Sheriff said, 'Nigra, you see that white lady standing there?' It was perfectly natural for me to say, 'No Sir. I don't see any white lady. I don't see color at all. I sees a human being.'"

"And when he cracked you upside the head with his brass knucks, it was perfectly natural for you to lay down and see all kinds of colors floatin in front of your eyes."

"If I remember correctly, he put a boot in your ass and invited you to join me on the ground. Then he begin his speech. 'We don't tolerate no silver rights niggers here in Mud Turtle. You wanna give a silver rights speech, we gots a tree that you can hang from and do your speech makin. Ant a tother thing, when a white lady is approaching a mud puddle, a nigger is supposed to lay down in it and let her step on his back so she don't get her shoes muddy. Ant a tother thing, you bet not look up her dress when she steppin over you.'"

"And then he blew his whistle and that big white heifer with her hair rolled up in a bun carrying three bags of Woolworth's loot, stepped right into the small part of my back."

"She must have weighed three hundred pounds and not an ounce less."

"And she had a little girl with her who weighed half her weight and decided to play a game of hopscotch between my ass and my shoulder blades."

"All we could do was crawl after that. Lucky there was a black man with a mule drawn wagon and he dropped us off to your aunt's place. She had the nerve to get mad because we forgot the stamp."

"You ever go back to Mud Turtle?"

"Never and wouldn't have gone back then if you hadn't brought up gas and crackers."

"Well, you brought up the midget."

"You brung Halle Berry in the story."

"Well, it started out being about a Turkey."

"And it ends being about a Turkey. Because a midget went into the Butchers' and a turkey came out minus a shoebox full of money."

"I wonder what happened in between that time?"

"We won't go into all of that. I've had enough of farting and turkeys and midgets."

The Road to Astroworld – Two Excerpts
Goose Steps

"Where you going, goose?"

Promise stopped. She had run through the gates of Paradise Gardens and was walking briskly down Lyon's Avenue with her head outstretched. Her Uncle Bobo and his friends loitered on the porch of a shotgun shack. The porch sagged like the inside of a boat. Two columns holding up the porch's roof leaned together. Bobo rested on his elbows between the posts stroking his chin with one hand as he eyed Promise. He held a Styrofoam cup in his other. His pals in frumpy clothes gathered around him grinning at her. One fellow wore a bus driver's dark blue uniform. His silver badge gleamed like a razor blade. A bright-green bottle sat on the banister shining under the sun's rays as if a jade offering. The men had taken a sip from the bottle. Their loins ached and they were ready for some female amusement. Promise put her foot on the bottom step and her hands on her hips.

The air was scented with rain, sweat, and the fruity wine. She looked at the grinning men and felt big inside. Their attention was on her and she acted "womanish" as Big Mama called it. At the same time, she turned her nose up at their "old men" clothes. They were at least thirty and they dressed foolish in her eyes. Not one of them was as "Fly" as Sugar Face in his glittering jackets and gold chains. Her favorite singer wouldn't be caught dead in a yellow suit or a T-shirt with a big black X on the front. And he sure wouldn't be caught near a shack drinking wine.

Part of her dismissed them, but still they were men and brought out the sass in her. She looked Bobo straight in the eye.

"Don't call me no goose."

"You was stepping mighty fast there, Pee. Big Mama ain't riding her broom behind you, is she?"

"You don't see her do you?"

"I ain't got to see her. I can tell she around by the way you flying down the street like a goose." Her uncle stuck his neck out and flapped his arms. The men laughed and slapped their legs. Promise frowned at Bobo's big belly shaking like a pillow. His thick ginger colored neck pushed aside the top button of his shirt and the collar opened like tiny wings around his face. When he laughed, his jaws puffed. "Pumpkin head," Promise thought. Her older brother Bobo had been nicknamed after this uncle and had the same large head. She was glad she wasn't a boy or named Bobo or else she might have a huge head too, she thought.

Promise peered over at her uncle's scooped-up-in-the-back red car parked in front of the house. A rear tire was missing a hubcap. She skipped to the car and peeked through the dark windows. Boxes hid under sheets in the rear as if they were playing hide and seek. A commode leaned over in the back seat.

"Why you have a nasty commode in your car, Bobo?" Promise asked scrunching up her nose.

"That's grown folk's business," he answered. The men snickered. "Besides, that commode is clean."

She caught the reflection of her hair in the tinted window. She smoothed her bangs and poked out her lips to check her imaginary lipstick. "Where Mr. Fritz's car? He done fired you for being drunk?" She asked observing Bobo and the men's faces in the glass.

The men glanced at Bobo and laughed. "Bobo, I didn't know you was married," one of them said.

"Watch out, Pee, I'll take my belt off."

"You do and your pants going to fall down. Where my Sugar Face CD and poster?"

"It's coming, Pee just like an ass whipping from Big Mama."

"Everything is always coming, including tickets to Astroworld. But, Big Mama says she going to beat you if you *come* to Jonathan's funeral smelling like wine."

"I'm a grown man little lady. Big Mama ain't beat my ass in thirty years. I'm still working on them tickets."

"Yeah, yeah," Promise sighed. She wrinkled her nose at the commode, turned, and skipped over to the porch.

"Where you supposed to be going anyway?" Bobo asked her.

"Down to Kwong's to buy some roses."

"Roses for what?"

"Mama's going to put them in Jonathan's coffin."

"Marsha and her ideas."

"It was Jonathan's idea."

Bobo looked at her for a moment. He shrugged and poured himself a drink. When he sat the bottle down, another hand reached for it.

"Bobo, I sure am sorry about your nephew."

"Thanks, man. Yeah, he was a good kid. Just got caught up in the wrong lifestyle." Bobo appeared as if he was going to spit.

"How he catch the AIDS?" Promise blurted out. Bobo cut his eyes at the men and then at her. Promise ducked her head. His red slits told her she had asked the wrong question. His friends stared down at their feet and up at the sun as if they were trying to figure out what it was. A woman in tight pants passed and the men craned their necks at her as if she was from the moon. Far off down the street there was a wailing of sirens. The men refilled their cups and glanced at each other to see who had something to say.

The man in the yellow suit cleared his throat. "Speaking of Mr. Fritz, Bobo, didn't the Leaky Eye get his wife?"

"Naw she slipped out of that nigga's greasy hands. You know she ain't no bigger than a matchstick and she just slipped out of his hands." Bobo answered and took a drink.

"She was lucky to get away. He killed one woman just down the street. I wonder why he kill some and let some live?"

"He'd kill 'em all if he had time."

"The nigga close to be found out. That's why he killin' the women now. He's desperate."

"You reckon he's a nigga, Bobo?"

"Fool, the news says he is. Besides, can't nothing white man sneak up in here and kill a black woman. Somebody would have seen him."

"The news can lie. A white man can put on black face paint and look just like a nigga. I seen a movie about that. I don't think the Leaky Eye is no nigga. I think he's a white man in blackface who got a thing for black women."

"Ain't nobody seen nothing white on the Leaky Eye."

"Well, I wouldn't reckon they be gazing at him with eyes wide open. He ain't going to let no woman stare at him like that. The women who do catch his eyes in the black dark, say he got gray eyes. Ain't none of us got gray eyes."

"Your Aunt, Susan got gray eyes, ain't she, Promise?" Bobo asked and nodded toward Promise. "Since you want to be all up in grown folks' conversation." Bobo knew Promise didn't care much for Susan.

Promise thought of her aunt's piercing gray eyes set in a face the color of school desks; and how those eyes stared and made her look at the floor. She studied a bug rather than answer him.

"Your Sister resembles a white woman, Bobo," the man in the yellow suit said. "Everybody say The Leaky Eye's face is like dirty dish water from them streaking eyes of his."

"A nigga on my job, got running gray eyes," Two Jack the Bus driver chimed in. "Guess what they call that nigga behind his back?"

"What?"

"Good coon."

"Now why they call him that?"

"'Cause you know how a coon wears a black mask—like a robber bandit? Well, this nigga look like he wearing a white mask sometimes. Some kind of chemical got throwed in his face when he was a boy. Burnt him all around his eyes. He wear shades all the time. Even when drive the bus at night."

"Why they let a half-blind nigga drive a bus?" Bobo asked. I bet he don't drive in the white neighborhoods. Shows how much white folks care about our asses. We got the Leaky Eye and a blind man driving a bus."

"Well, I didn't say he was blind. The bus company got regulations." Two Jack defended.

"Fuck regulations. Maybe that nigga is the Leaky Eye."

"Hell no, that nigga scared of women. His wife got a ring in his nose as big as that hub cap laying there." He nodded toward a hubcap lying in the gutter. "He come to work with knots upside his head and his face scratched up like a chicken got to him. I know he ain't no rapist."

"The New Brotherhood is on patrol gunning for The Leaky Eye," the man with the X on his shirt spoke up.

"Them niggas ain't shit," Bobo spat.

"Aw I wouldn't say that," Neck said directly to Bobo

"Why? Because you a member?"

"The New Brotherhood comes direct from the old Black Panthers."

"What good did they do? What happened to the so-called revolution? Cops and the FBI ended that shit."

"Well, I take exception, Bobo. I think the Panthers did a lot of good. Made us proud to be black men for one."

"Where that nigga at on your shirt?" Bobo pointed to the picture of Malcolm X frowning between the large Black X crisscrossing Neck's T-shirt.

"Well..."

"Well, my ass. Anytime we try to rise up, the man puts his foot on our necks. As long as we kill or rape each other, he don't give a shit. That's why these gangs everywhere and that Leaky Eye bastard is roaming all over. When he touch a white woman, the cops gonna find him quicker than stink finds shit. Mark my words. New Brotherhood my ass."

"Why he like to raise up women's dresses, Bobo?" Promised blurted.

The men stirred uncomfortably and sought out the sky once again.

"Promise you ask one more question—you hear me little girl?" You worse than a cop. Just stick close to home so he don't try to raise your dress up."

"You watch, Leaky Eye is going to look like a white man from the old-timey minstrel shows," the man in yellow said. He didn't bother to pour his drink. He took a hit straight from the bottle. The others followed suit. "You gonna see. He gonna look like a greasy devil. He greasy. That's why Fritz's wife slipped out from him. I wish she could have seen his belly or his ass. We'd know the truth then."

"I wonder what a fine black woman like her see in Fritz?" Two Jack the bus driver asked. "He's bald and pink as a baby."

"Well shit, just open your eyes," Bobo answered. All of us collected together couldn't come up with five-thousand dollars if our asses depended on it. If my Mama hadn't had that dollar a week burial policy, you think Marsha could have buried her boy? Hell no. And I ain't got no money. Fritz's stocks and other crooked shit he's in earn five thousand in a day. I drive that motherfucker around every day to five different banks. You hear me? Five!" Bobo spread his fingers out like a fan.

"He ought to have let you use his car today for the funeral," the man in yellow drawled. "Could have saved y'all some money.

"I sure as hell asked him and he sure as hell told me no. Marsha had to pay extra for a limousine. Or else I would have had to drive my family members in that raggedy shit. Stingy motherfucker." Bobo spat toward his car. "He don't want a bunch of niggas in his car."

"Well, that wife of his sure is a nigga." The man in the yellow suit said.

"She don't think so because she's from Brazil somewhere."

"Money ain't everything," Neck retorted. His Adam's apple bobbed as if he were swallowing an egg. "Five Fritzes couldn't equal the size of my you-know-what and couldn't match the motion of my ocean lapping between some big brown thighs."

"Aw Neck, women ain't thinking about all of that these days. Cold cash rules the world."

"I bet they thinks about plenty when Leaky Eye is going to town on them. Woo! Wee!" He grabbed and held his crotch.

"Nigga, you sound like you rootin' for the Leaky Eye."

"He doing what we ought to be doing, except we ought to be doing it to white women. You ever try to get with Fritz's wife?"

"Hell no, not that scrawny ass thing."

"I bet she misses her a good black man in the midnight hour."

"She got plenty of fur coats to remind her of our black asses. He don't let me drive her unless he's in the car. She drive her own self in that Jag he bought her."

"I'd drive her. I'd drive her right out of them furs and jewels. Drive her into my kitchen cookin' some beans, rice, and pork chops. Fatten her ass up."

Promise stared at Neck's bobbling throat as she listened to him drawl. Neck winked at her and smiled, showing off a mouth of crooked gold teeth. Promise looked off.

"Well, I better get on down the road a piece. Sorry 'bout your nephew, Bobo," he said slipping off the porch like a snake. He glanced at Promise and winked.

"I don't like him," Promise said as Neck got halfway up the walkway. "He got something stuck in his throat and he nasty."

"Probably a chicken bone," the man in the yellow suit said. "Y'all ever seen that nigga eat fried chicken? Don't be nothing left but the box it came in."

"Yeah, I bet that ain't all he can swallow with a neck like his. They tell me him and your Neph…" The bus driver stopped midway his sentence.

Bobo and the man in the yellow suit stared at Two Jack. Bobo stood straight up.

"Him and my nephew what, nigga?

"Nothing, Bobo, nothing at all."

Bobo glared at Two Jack. Two Jack shifted from one foot to the other. He looked at the man in yellow who gazed down the Avenue. Promise stared at him. He glanced down at his feet.

"I say let's have a drink to nothing," the man in the yellow suit said as he slapped Bobo and Two Jack on their backs.

"Don't let your tongue outrun your brains, nigga," Bobo said taking his eyes off Two Jack to reach for the bottle. "Yeah, let's have a drink to nothing," He spat.

"Whatever the Leaky Eye is, one thing is for sure," said the man in the yellow suit, "He's slippery as an eel."

"Slippery for sure. One woman said he had on white and got her in a cemetery in the back of a hearse. Another said he had on a Bus driver's uniform." Their eyes fell on Two Jack.

"What the hell y'all gazing at me for?" Two Jack asked. "I told you about that nigga with them runny eyes."

"We just saying what we heard like you said what you heard," Bobo replied.

"Whoever it is," said the man in the yellow suit, "He's a tiger who can change his stripes."

After a few more hits from the bottle, Bobo observed Promise sprawled on the bottom step.

"Say Pee, who dressed you this morning? Got you looking like Raggedy Ann with them bunny shoes, wedding dress, and yellow shorts."

"It ain't no wedding dress."

"I'd say Nettie dressed you."

"Nettie ain't dressed nobody. Mama is dressing her after she clean the slobber off her face. Besides, I ain't going to no funeral this morning. I'm going to Astroworld."

"Astroworld? Pee is you crazy? I told you I was gonna get some tickets."

Promise shrugged. She got up and studied a poster stapled to a tree. The poster had the same X and frowning man that was printed on Neck's shirt.

"Besides, Pee, the school buses are gone already. We saw them leave earlier. How you going to get to Astroworld?" Bobo asked.

Promise glanced at Bobo and his friends grinning at her. She hunched her shoulders. She remembered Mr. Wick holding up the red stop sign and the buses crawling away from the school. There came a rumbling and snorting behind her. She turned around just as a yellow and white city bus passed. The bus's large tires churned through a puddle of water and splashed Bobo's car. Promise snapped her fingers.

"I'm going to catch a city bus."

"Promise, you ain't never caught a bus by yourself in your life. But I bet you catching some crawfish with your toes right now."

Promise shot a glance at the puddle soaking through her bunny slippers. Her mouth opened for a moment then quickly shut. She snatched her feet out of the water and sidled over to Bobo's car pretending to be interested in the commode in the back.

"Look at little Miss Nettie who don't know how to stay out of mud puddles," Bobo hissed at her. The back of Promise's neck warmed as anger washed over her. A tear trickled out of the corner of her eye. She wiped her face with her sleeve, turned from the car, and started down the street.

"Big Mama say you better have your pants pulled up and don't be showing your dirty drawers at the funeral," she said as she trotted off with her nose in front of her. The men on the porch heehawed. A passing car drowned her uncle's voice. Down the sidewalk, Kwong's Market squatted like a red cinder block.

Promise kicked a tin can and sent it rolling. The can came to rest in a patch of grass. She raised her foot to kick it again and a strip of yellow police tape twitching like a cat's tail caught her eye. She followed the tape's trail over broken glass and beer cans. The end was attached to a dwelling hiding behind a clump of bushes. The house sat far from the street as if it didn't want to be bothered with anything happening on Lyon's Avenue. It leaned against two planks bracing its right side. A mass of posters on its left side stuck to it like swatch of bandages. In the front yard, the weeds lay flat as if a giant foot had stomped them. A large hole pierced the wall next to the front door and two huge planks were nailed crisscross the opening. Police tape fluttered meekly from the hole like streamers from a long-ago party. Promise made one step forward and stopped. She thought of all the talk about the Leaky Eye floating around—*"he sleeps curled up in empty houses like a snake," "he hangs from the ceiling like a bat," "the liquid from his eyes burns you like acid..."* She stood under a tree and observed her uncle and his friends. They laughed and passed the green bottle around. They had forgotten about her. She turned, picked up a dried-out stick, and crept into the yard. The ground softened by the morning rain, was littered with paper and tin cans. Rags blotted the yard like wet skins. A hospital gurney leaned on its side propped up by a chinaberry tree. Its legs stuck out like metal bones. Promise struck the gurney and it answered her with a dull clang. She hid behind an abandoned icebox and peeped in case a head popped up in the window to see who had made the noise. The windows remained dark and silent. Promise let out her breath.

"Hey, hey," she called out. Leaves shimmied in the wind. She shouted more "heys" before stepping on the porch and peeping through the hole. The darkness was sliced by slivers of light, let in through gaps in the planks. A pile of rags took up one corner. A rusty box spring with a blue rubber glove tangled in its coils rested on the floor. Footprints covered the dusty floor as if people had been dancing. As she peered at the ceiling to check for bats, Promise heard a scraping noise in the yard. She yanked her head out of the hole and turned. Neck stood in the yard watching. The thing in his throat moved if he were swallowing.

"What you doing up in here, little Mama?" he drawled.

"Ain't doing nothing."

"Aw, you doing something all right." Neck started toward the porch, stepped in some muck, and cursed under his breath. He stomped his foot on a rock to loosen the mud and scraped his feet on the bottom step as he walked up the porch. Promise backed away and stood watching as he poked his head in the hole. He pulled himself through the hole, or rather the hole sucked him in one leg bone and one arm bone at a time. Clouds of dust danced near his feet as he kicked trash and debris. Promise watched him bend and pull the glove from the box spring. He held it up to a shard of light and scratched his finger over the rubber. He examined his fingernail.

"Blood." He stared at Promise and threw the glove on the floor. He continued poking around. "You know who was in this house the other day?" Promise shrugged. "The Leaky Eye had him a woman in here. The police wore that glove when they examined her body. Woo! Wee!" He screeched. "I know she had a time with his business. Woo! Wee!"

He looked back at the hole where Promise had stood moments before. It was empty. Promise didn't stop running until she stumbled into the legs of some boys dribbling and passing a basketball between them.

"Watch out, Little Mama," one boy said as he steadied Promise by her shoulders. She peeped around the boy's waist as Neck stepped out of the yard. He stopped in the middle of the street and stared in her direction before he continued to the other side and disappeared between two row houses. Promise threw away the stick she had been holding and continued down the street. Her shoulder brushed against a smooth surface. She stopped and frowned. It was the garish red mural picturing the smiling Kwong family. Their large teeth made her feel as if she was about to be attacked by a pack of monkeys. When she was smaller, Jonathan had to hold her hand or she would run into the street to get away from the mural. Promise reached her hand upward as if she expected Jonathan to grab it. Then she remembered she was alone.

Dear LaKeisha Ann:

Do you remember that rainy day, when the rain trapped you in my house, (when the rain was to me like Christmas tinsel and not razor blades), and we played husband and wife? Do you remember that day? My Big Mama dozed in front of the TV as "Another World" flickered in front of her closed eyes. Jonathan snoozed. The sheets formed a tent from his erection. We watched that tent rise and fall in time with his breathing. I didn't know then, but now I know why we all of a sudden wanted to play husband and wife. The rain fills people with romantic notions. That's why I can forgive a certain bus driver.

We argued over who was going to be the husband coming in from the rain from working hard on the job. You won when you said the husband had to be a boy. Why I thought a woman could be a husband, I don't know. I didn't want to be no boy.

You wore my mother's colander for a hard hat and a "Ninja Turtles" lunch kit was your toolbox. You went outside on the front porch and stood for a few minutes while I pretended to be the wife inside the house washing dishes. You kept coming in before your time and I had to keep sending you out.

"Wait a minute, boy . . . I'm washing dishes . . . No, you can't come in yet, I'm watching 'The Young and the Restless' . . . Okay, now you can come in 'cause I'm cooking your supper . . ."

You came in and pecked me on the cheek, looked in my pot at the imaginary beans and rice and said they smelled good. Then you said you had to get out of your wet clothes. I said "you can't get naked in the kitchen. You got to go in the bathroom or the bedroom." And you said, "where they at?" And I said, "silly husband, you don't know where your bedroom or bathroom is?" You twisted my arm and made me tell you.

Behind a big old blue vinyl dinette chair where Big Mama had some red flowerpots, was the bathroom. You said you had never seen a red commode. I said pretend it's white. Underneath the kitchen table was our bedroom.

You went into the "bathroom" and took off all of your clothes for real and pretended to take a shower. I stopped cooking to look at you. You said, "Woman, you can't see when I'm taking a shower because there's a wall there." I said, "the wall fell down. Our bad children knocked it down." You said, okay you was going to whip them when you got out of the shower. So, you got through showering and put a dish towel around your waist and came back into the kitchen and asked which one of our children knocked down the wall? I pointed to my dolls and said all of them did. You told the dolls "I'm going to whip you for knocking down that wall." All the dolls that had on panties, you pulled their panties off and spanked them with your hand. The ones that didn't have on panties, you whipped them harder with an extension cord because they were nasty for not wearing panties and had been doing the "nasty" with some boys.

Then you tried to whip me with the extension cord. But I

told you, you couldn't whip me like that because I was a grown woman and your wife. You said okay, but I got to beat you 'cause you let the children tear down the wall and you don't have my supper ready. And I said okay, but a man beats a lady with his fists. You pushed me around and pretended to give me a black eye. I found a Magic marker and drew a half moon under my eye. After you beat me, I went out on the porch and acted like I was crying. You came out on the porch still wearing our dish towel. I forgot we was playing and said, "Girl, you can't come out on the porch in a dish towel!" You said a man can go on the porch in a towel or his drawers as long as he ain't naked. I said, Okay.

I pretended to cry some more. I said I was going to go to a woman's shelter. You said baby come back in the house. I'm sorry I beat you. So, we hugged and made up and we went back into the house and I finished cooking your supper. You sat down at the table in the dish towel. I said hold on wait a minute, you can't sit at the table in a towel in front of the children. You said I'm a man, I can do whatever I want. And I said I'm the woman of the house, and I say a man has to be dressed when he eats in front of the children. You never see the daddy on the "Cosby Show" eating in a towel in front of his children. And he don't beat his wife. You said yes, he do when nobody's looking.

I started to cry for real and said, "Please LaKeisha Ann, play fair! You never want to do things the way I want to do them. And you said, "Shut up, silly bitch. I don't want to be your husband anyway. Next thing, you'll want me to put a carrot between my legs and poke you in your snatch."

You whipped off the dishtowel, put on your clothes, and went home. The sun came out and painted the kitchen gold. But all I could do was sit down at the table and cry. I cried and the dolls cried too because they wanted their Daddy. And ever since that day I've been curious about carrots. They served some here the other day and it made me think of you.

Love,

Promise

P S. I told the story to Big Fingers, and he said a carrot is a poor substitute for a man, but he like the part about us playing husband and wife.

Excerpt from Into the Water, a Short Story

Once inside Jill's apartment, Alvin pulled off his shades. The dark glasses were his mannish way of being cool, and his childish idea of assuming they hid him from watchful eyes. His chin was a little on the long side with a pinhead nick in the center. The cheekbones sat high, and his slight overbite made his appear more boyish than his eighteen years. He tried to disguise his baby face with sideburns that looked like iron shavings on his smooth caramel face. He stood in the kitchen of Jill's two-room efficiency listening to the water trickling through the guts of her refrigerator. The tinkling reminded him of Jill peeing in the toilet after they had made love. He took a deep breath, grabbed his crotch, and stepped into her bedroom. Streaks of moonlight streamed through the tightly drawn blinds and sliced the bed and floor before disappearing under a table. Alvin slung a plastic bag onto the table next to Jill's bed. Cookies a small square white cake, potato chips, canned tuna, and two bottles of beer hit the wood surface like a hammer and scattered her pills. Her artificial arm almost hit the floor.

Excerpt from David, Jonathan, and Sylvester

Old Mother Earth changes as she rolls through the heavens and the times change with her. Nineteen sixty-five came, and David and other *Negroes* could eat their hot dogs at Woolworth's and Kress's lunch counter. Young black men and black women walked with their noses just as high in the air as David's. And they weren't even rich. The bank took down its colored entrance. The Negro college and Negro hospital took the Negro out of their names and Riverside General and Texas Southern University respectively. In fact, Negroes stopped being Negroes. David was no fool. He kept those big ears tuned to white men's talk. He took advantage of his stool at the Woolworth's lunch counter and listened. Many despaired over the way the world was turning. Some men talked of the day when the dollar would become as worthless as toilet paper. "Gold. We got to go back to the gold standard," David overheard one fellow say. David had gold, gold in his rings and a nearly solid gold watch. He patronized Levitz's Jewelers religiously. But he would need more gold in case his money became worthless due to Russian Communists or race riots.

"David, this is the fifth gold watch you've bought this month. What's going on?" David's bad leg trembled, and he couldn't keep his feet still. Simon sounded like the law and David didn't like a Jew sounding like the law to him. Yet David demurred and looked down. His slicked back hair filled Simon's polished saucer sized glasses.

"I need the gold," David said quietly.

"You need gold? What you need gold for?"

"Communists."

Simon Levitz looked at David a long time. David had been his best Negro customer, actually his best customer period for many years. In fact, he had sold David his first diamond ring while Levitz was a Pawn Shop at the foot of the Fannin Street Bridge near the bayou. David was the first black customer to enter the store when they moved to Main Street near the big banks. Simon credited David for bringing in the black trade. *If Big Nose David Calloway bought his rings from Levitz's, then they must be good.* But David was no jeweler. Not even his big eyes were big enough to see the flaws of those "*flawless*" diamond rings. But the fact that he was able to spend his money in Levitz's chandeliered store made him happy.

David looked up when he thought he heard Simon choking. But Simon was laughing so hard he was crying. David's belly began to boil, and he felt the urge to knock the Jew to the floor. Probably would have done so, if Levitz was still a Pawn Shop close to the muddy bayou and not on Main Street in the heart of steel and glass, well dressed white people, and cops. Simon stopped when he saw that David wasn't laughing nor smiling. He sobered.

"David, David, no no, no. That's not the way to buy gold. If you're worried about the state of the world, you buy bullion."

"Bullion?" David thought of soup and wondered what foolishness was about to come from Simon's mouth. Simon was surely going to be the second white man he had ever hit, after he had had to rough up that wino he used as a surrogate to buy his stocks.

"Yes, gold bullion. Gold coins. I only got a couple of gold coins here in necklaces, but you need to go see my Brother-in-law Izak. He's got a coin and bullion shop way out Westheimer Road. He'll fix you up."

Soon David's safe deposit boxes filled with South African Krugerrands. He shouted down anyone at Joe's Barbershop who questioned his loyalty to his African brethren.

"Hell, I ain't never been to South Africa. The south United States is enough for me. What them white folks do to them jungle niggers ain't my business. They ought to get them a Martin Luther King like we got over here if they suffering so."

The afroed and dashiki clad young looked at David and shook their heads.

"You sound worse than the pigs, man—worse than the pigs."

David stewed and wished for his long-gone gun and official badge. His crippled leg pained him and put him on a cane. All a man had to do was kick that leg and send David crashing to the ground.

About the Author

Charles W. Harvey is a native Houstonian and a graduate of the University of Houston. Charles was a 1st place prize recipient of PEN/Discovery for Cheeseburger, which went on to be published in the Ontario Review. Harvey was also awarded the Cultural Arts Council of Houston Grant for Writers and Artists. Charles has been published in *Soulfires*, *Story Magazine*, *SHADE*, *High Infidelity*, *The James White Review,* and recently *NEWVERSENEWS*. He is the author of the novels "The Butterfly Killer," "The Road to Astroworld," and "Antoine's Double Trouble." He is also the author of several story and poetry collections.

Other Books of Note

Connect with Wes Writers

Website[1]

Twitter[2]

Facebook[3]

The Publisher and Authors from Wes Writers & Publishers[4] strive to bring you the best in fiction and poetry. We support many fine author/brands and diverse fiction genres. We strive for excellence. A better reading experience won't happen without your valuable input. That's why reviews are so helpful. Please take the time and leave a review. We also want to stay in touch with you. The best way to do so is to join our mailing list. By joining, you will get excerpts from our upcoming titles and other important information about books and publishing. Please subscribe to the mailing list. Thank you. Subscribe[5]

---

1. https://www.charlesharveyauthor.wordpress.com/

2. https://twitter.com/CharlesHarvey99

3. https://www.facebook.com/pages/Wes-Writers-Publishers/200150716671422

4. http://charlesharveyauthor.wordpress.com/

5. https://subscribepage.io/9sPXo5

Don't miss out!

Visit the website below and you can sign up to receive emails whenever Charles Harvey publishes a new book. There's no charge and no obligation.

https://books2read.com/r/B-A-EWG-UYDR

BOOKS 2 READ

Connecting independent readers to independent writers.

Did you love *Urban Tales*? Then you should read *Antoine's Double Trouble*[6] by Charles Harvey!

Antoine Rucker, a young twenty-something Black IT executive leads a double life. During the day, he works for a major insurance company in Downtown Atlanta. On weekend nights, he hustles on the street turning tricks near the infamous "Bulldogs Bar." He's smart, a graduate of Morehouse College and is being groomed as his company's new CIO (Chief Information Officer) What drives him to the streets and into the arms of misfit and wounded men? Will Antoine's sordid nightlife catch up with him? Will he ever get the monkey off his back?

Excerpt:

The next morning when I got up to use the restroom, I heard my Mother in the study. I walked to the door and stood watching

---

6. https://books2read.com/u/bzpWLj

7. https://books2read.com/u/bzpWLj

as she kneeled scrubbing the wall along the baseboards. My stomach quivered. I felt like a little boy caught doing something wrong. She sensed my presence and turned around.

"A rat pissed on this wall. Before you leave, I want you to buy some poison and put down some traps. I told John there were rats in this house. But nooo, he didn't believe me. And when he finally saw one, you know what he said?" She looked at me. I shrugged. "He said they were God's creatures. If Noah could tolerate two, we can tolerate one." She laughed. "That man was a mess."

The belt lay on top of the desk, where I had left it. Mama continued scrubbing the wall and talking to herself. "I will not have rats in my house. He would leave me to have to deal with this, do what he should have done when he was alive. Rats pissing all over everything, just like his sisters think they're going to piss all over me."

I picked up the belt. "Why didn't you stop him, Mama?"

"Oh you know, your Father was as stubborn as ten mules. If that man didn't want to do something, he didn't do it."

"Not the rats--this."

She looked at me holding the belt in my hand. "What are you talking about?"

"You know what I'm talking about."

Mama looked away, dipped her sponge in the bucket, and sloshed sudsy water on the wall. She ignored the mess she made on her pants. "Put that thing away. Your Father is dead. Let him rest in peace."

Get it Now!

Original Title: Boy For Hire

Read more at https://charlesharveyauthor.wordpress.com.

Also by Charles Harvey

Astroworld
Promise: Short Stories From The Road to Astroworld
Promise's Letters From the Road to Astroworld

Buck Wile Stories
Buck Wile is Punk'd Out On Da Downlow
Buck Wile is Butt Naked In Da City

Dogs Bark
When Dogs Bark the Short Story
Bark Too

Poetic Journeys
Americana
3AM - Poems and Stories From the Other Mind
The Last Supper
Rough Cut Until I Bleed

Roommates
Roommates and The Old Dead Seaman
Roommates and Other Stories

Standalone
Betty's House
Black Queen
The Blue Train To Heaven
The Power Plant
Ebenezer Jenkins' Christmas in Chicago
Q is a Bad Letter and Other QQ Crazy Stories
Catnip Gray Cat Detective: The Tabitha Davenport Affair
Antoine's Double Trouble
Maura And Her Two Husbands
Urban Tales
Into The Water, A Short Story
David, Jonathan, and Sylvester
Cheeseburger and Other Stories
A Foursome Plus Poems
Kiss and Say Goodbye

Watch for more at https://charlesharveyauthor.wordpress.com.

About the Author

Charles W. Harvey is a native Houstonian and a graduate of the University of Houston. At UofH he studied fiction under the guidance of Rosellen Brown and Chitra Divakaruni. In 1987, Charles was a 1st place prize recipient of PEN/Discovery for his short story Cheeseburger, which went on to be published in the Ontario Review. In 1989 Charles Harvey was awarded the Cultural Arts Council of Houston Grant for Writers and Artists. Also in 1989 he was a finalist in the MacDonald's Literary Achievement Awards. Charles has been published in Soulfires, Story Magazine SHADE, High Infidelity, The James White Review, and others. He is the author of the novels The Butterfly Killer, The Road to Astroworld, and Antoine's Double Trouble. He is also the author of several story and poetry collections. He also writes for the stage and screen.

Read more at https://charlesharveyauthor.wordpress.com.

About the Publisher

Wes Writers and Publishers strives to bring you great books for your reading pleasure. We have been in the business of producing quality works of fiction for over two decades. We will branch out in the future to add more authors to bring you the reader, very high quality and entertaining stories from all genres. It begins with Charles W. Harvey our star prize winning literary writer an poet. He is the author of the prize winning short story Cheeseburger selected by Joyce Carol Oates in the 1987 PEN/Southwest Prize. He is a frequent participant in NANOWRIMO and other literary endeavors. Please feel free to sample his many stories and two Novels via Smashwords and other fine retailers. AC Adams brings you a little something different. He is our premier author for the gay literary erotica genre. Many of our readers have enjoyed his Roommates series. Look forward for a lot more to come from this up and coming author. Clarissa Haley comes from east Texas. She likes quirky little stories that swim around that brain of hers. She has several exciting projects in the works. She has a few romance stories in the works for future release Wes Writers and Publishers (we like being called WWP) will be adding more l writers under its wings in the near future. We love good stories.

Read more at https://charlesharveyauthor.wordpress.com.

www.ingramcontent.com/pod-product-compliance
Lightning Source LLC
Chambersburg PA
CBHW062145150726

47991CB00006B/2178